Galen stared at Honor, bewildered. "You're not making any sense. I'm not working any evil."

"You know what you've done," she said in a deadly tone. "Don't pretend you haven't worked some enchantment."

He spread his arms. "*What* enchantment?"

She wasn't listening to him. "I can feel it even now. Strange, maddening sensations. And the heat. It crawls through me whenever you appear. I know it's your doing, because the closer you come, the hotter the flames."

Galen studied her; indignation made her seem even more appealing than usual. "Damnation and sin," he said softly. "You really think I've worked a spell on you." He drew nearer. "My sweet little sunset, what you're experiencing is desire, unaided by magic of any sort." He placed his lips close to her ear and breathed the words, "Plain, ordinary lust."

She gasped. "It is not, and you're an evil-minded, corrupt man to say such a thing."

Galen laughed and shook his head, then slipped his arm around her waist and drew her to him. Caught off guard, she froze and stared up at him. He dragged her against him so that their lips almost touched.

"If you don't believe me, I'll have to prove it to you."

Bantam Books by Suzanne Robinson

THE LEGEND

JUST BEFORE MIDNIGHT

THE TREASURE

THE RESCUE

HEART OF THE FALCON

THE ENGAGEMENT

LORD OF THE DRAGON

LORD OF ENCHANTMENT

LADY DANGEROUS

LADY VALIANT

LADY DEFIANT

LADY HELLFIRE

LADY GALLANT

*and her romantic short story
in the Bantam Anthology*

WHEN YOU WISH . . .

THE LEGEND

SUZANNE ROBINSON

BANTAM BOOKS

New York Toronto London
Sydney Auckland

THE LEGEND

PUBLISHING HISTORY
Bantam paperback edition / March 2001

ISBN 0-553-57964-9

Published simultaneously in the United States and Canada

Bantam Books are published by Bantam Books, a division of
Random House, Inc. Its trademark, consisting of the words "Bantam
Books" and the portrayal of a rooster, is Registered in U.S. Patent
and Trademark Office and in other countries. Marca Registrada.
Bantam Books, 1540 Broadway, New York, New York 10036.

PRINTED IN THE UNITED STATES OF AMERICA

OPM   10 9 8 7 6 5 4 3 2 1

This book is dedicated to Nita Taublib
in appreciation for her faith in my writing.
Nita, you took a chance on me, and
I'll never forget your support.

The moon floated in a silver mist in a sky full of glittering stars. A cloud sailed across the bright orb like a slow distant ship on the ocean. He closed his eyes for a moment, and when he opened them, the cloud had vanished into a great bank of thunderheads. Galen knew there would be no sleep for him this night.

The same vision had awakened him countless times for nearly three months now. Galen was used to visions. He and his brothers had inherited special gifts from their mother, a dark-haired, fey Welsh noblewoman, skills that they'd hidden from the world for fear of being accused of witchcraft. Having reached the age of thirty-two, Galen had become skilled at interpreting the visions. Sometimes they referred to the distant past and meant little to him, but this one was different. It was about the future of the royal family, and it was about his friend, Edward, King of England.

The vision always began the same way. He felt himself transformed into a raven, black, gimlet-eyed, and fierce. He flew high above the ground, guided by a bright ribbon of water. Rolling emerald hills and fields of barley and grass floated beneath him until he came to a cluster of buildings upon the bank of the river. He recognized the spires and buttresses of Westminster below him. Tiny boats and river taxis dodged between slow-moving barges and larger sailing vessels. He flew on past Charing Cross, and glimpsed the Fleet River, then St. Paul's Cathedral, followed by Saltwharf,

Dowgate, and London Bridge. As he sailed over Billingsgate, he glimpsed a soaring white tower surrounded by high defensive walls. He knew this was home, for in his dream he was one of the fabled Tower ravens.

He angled down, gliding rapidly over the ring walls, past the Bell Tower, St. Thomas's Tower, and Traitor's Gate. Swerving, he flapped his wings and then dove for one of the projecting towers in the great white keep that dominated Tower Hill. Then the vision changed; he changed. One moment he was flapping hard, trying to land on a crenel, and the next he was in the chapel, facing its elongated nave. He stood, suddenly a man on a man's legs, in the vast chamber with its massive rounded arches supported by thick pillars. He looked up at the tribune gallery above the arches, and there glimpsed a shadow as it flitted from archway to archway.

The shadow exuded evil. Galen felt an overwhelming urge to follow it, and he raced up to the gallery, through a narrow doorway, and up a flight of winding stairs in one of the towers that formed the corners of the keep. The shadow moved with supernatural speed, darted around a bend in the stair and stopped at an unguarded door. Without aid, the door swung open with a long, moaning creak, and the shadow floated across the threshold.

Galen stopped several steps below, for the closer he came to the mysterious shadow, the more fearful he became. His heart was drumming hard against his ribs. His skin was clammy, and he trembled with a terror that emanated from his wildly beating heart. He forced his foot to move to the next step and the next until he reached the doorway. Inching his head around the door molding, he peered inside a small chamber with a vaulted ceiling and a tester bed draped with damask hangings embroidered with the royal coat of arms. The hangings had been shoved aside to reveal two boys with golden hair who so resembled the king that he knew they had to be the sons of Edward Plantagenet.

Without warning, the shadow separated itself from the darkness around the bed. By the time it reached the boys it had coalesced into the shape of a man, and in the man's hand a pillow. Galen tried to move, but his legs had grown as heavy as lead boulders. As he struggled, the man lowered the pillow over the boys' faces. Galen shouted as he watched the pillow being pressed over the boys' mouths, but no sound came out. He struggled there, horrified and helpless, as the small bodies writhed.

Then, suddenly, Galen was jolted out of his human body, back into the form of a raven, the remnants of terror still clinging to him like the putrid flesh of a corpse. In an instant he was flying over a battlefield where two armies fought, one under the king's banner bearing the white rose of York, the other under the red rose of Lancaster. He spied the damascened armor of the king, its helmet closed, obscuring his face. Galen landed in a leafless tree as the battle raged. He couldn't see what happened to the king, but he heard the screams from men around him. Lancastrian foes surrounded a Yorkist knight, closed in, and stabbed him viciously. Galen stretched his wings, struggling to find his hands while the bloody attack continued. The knight screamed, and he screamed back, and that was when Galen woke.

Galen shook his head and rubbed his eyes, trying to rid himself of the evil vision. He hated his gift of sight, and he'd prayed to God to deliver him from what he could only see as a curse. His prayers had gone unanswered. Experience had taught him that acting upon matters so far out of his hands could only yield tragedy. He'd sworn never to rush into action on account of his gift, for once, long ago, he'd done just that and caused the death of his wife and children.

No, if he tried to prevent the events foretold in the vision, he could very well hasten the deaths of those two boys. In any case, his visions didn't always come to pass. The future was fluid and susceptible to many forces beyond his comprehension. But this vision was persistent, and unlike most, came only at night. It robbed him of sleep and made his waking hours an ordeal and had driven him to seek the solitude of Durance Guarde before he betrayed himself and his gift at the intrigue-ridden court of Edward IV.

Galen de Marlowe drew the black robe closer about his body. His brothers were furious with him for vanishing to this remote, deserted ruin on the edge of his demesne, but Galen needed time to master this disturbing vision. It troubled and frightened him, and if he didn't overcome it soon, he feared it might become stronger than he and take over his life.

Galen glanced around the chamber, at the bare stone walls and chilly, worn floorboards, and wondered why he'd been drawn to this place. He hadn't thought about Durance Guarde in years. He and Sir Walter Stafford should have settled the question of who owned the holding, but neither of them had considered the matter important. Galen was certain the place was part of the de Marlowe lands, but he had no desire to fight about it. After all, no one wanted to live here. Peasants avoided it, refused to travel near the old ruin unless forced to for reasons. When Galen's manservant, Ralph, had heard where they were going, he'd protested as if his master proposed to spend a few months in hell.

But Galen had needed a refuge, and Durance Guarde had popped into his thoughts like a cuckoo invading the nest of an unsuspecting bird. Once the image of the isolated ruin had lodged his thoughts, he couldn't rid himself of it. Why was he so drawn to the place? It wasn't just that Durance Guarde was deserted and provided privacy. And why did it make him so wary? Could it be that the old legend troubled him? Great evil had been wrought in this place.

No, it didn't make sense, for at the same time he felt safe at Durance Guarde. He felt comforted here, and ever since he'd arrived he'd experienced a strange sense of excitement, a tingling expectation. But then the excitement would vanish as suddenly as it had come upon him.

Still restless, Galen rose and returned to the window, weary with trying to unravel mysteries. There were only two things of which he was certain—he needed refuge from court to make sense of this burden of a vision that wouldn't leave, and that refuge had to be Durance Guarde. Certainly the reputation of the place didn't frighten him. His gift made him too familiar with the mysterious side of life to allow old legends to scare him. The stories of Durance Guarde were told to frighten children and ignorant peasants. He'd been in more battles than he cared to remember, and in them lay real hells, and horrors to make the devil scream. No, ghosts didn't frighten him. Besides, the events here had taken place so long ago. Galen leaned against the wall beside the window and tried to recall what he knew.

A line of hills separated the Stafford and de Marlowe lands, and upon the tallest of these sat the ruined castle of Durance Guarde. It was said that there had been a fortification at Durance Guarde since Roman times, and that in Saxon times a timber structure replaced the old Roman fort. Berengar de Villard, a descendent of the Norman invaders, built a new stone keep and

defensive wall around the year 1220. And that was
when the trouble started.

More outlaw than nobleman, Berengar grew rich
by robbing those who passed through his demesne.
For years he attacked wealthy merchants and mi-
nor nobles, robbed them and often killed them.
Sometimes he dragged them back to Durance
Guarde and threw them in the dungeon, where
they remained in windowless cells and oubliettes,
forgotten, until they starved to death. His favorite
evening amusement was torturing his prisoners.

Berengar slaughtered a party escorting a beautiful girl, Lady Rowena Seve, to her betrothal. He
abducted Rowena, violated her and held her prisoner for long days, which stretched into weeks,
and Rowena became increasingly desperate. One
terrible night Berengar and his men were celebrat-
ing a rich haul. The castle fell silent when everyone passed out from drink, and Berengar spent
most of the night using Rowena. When her captor
fell into a drunken stupor, Rowena rose up from
the bed, stole his dagger and stabbed him. She
missed his heart and Berengar managed to pull the
dagger from his shoulder. In a rage he chased
Rowena up the stairs of the tower in which she'd
been held. Driven to madness by her ordeal, with
Berengar right behind her, she raced to the roof
and plunged to her death.

It is said that a few weeks later Berengar woke to
hear the sound of a woman weeping in the tower at
night, just as Rowena used to weep when she was

alive. Soon Berengar was too afraid to sleep in his room, and he moved to one in the larger tower from which Rowena's Tower projected. There he didn't hear the weeping, and he rested well. He never used his dagger again, and locked it in the treasury in another tower.

Nevertheless, people still heard the crying if they went near Rowena's chamber. Berengar continued his evil ways, growing even more drunken and violent when people began to see a glowing, ephemeral image of a young woman on the roof of the smaller tower late at night. A year passed, and the first anniversary of Rowena's death arrived. Berengar drank heavily and refused to go near Rowena's Tower.

Late that night, he fell into a drunken sleep in his own tower, only to wake to the sound of weeping. There at the foot of his bed stood Rowena's glowing figure. She held a dagger and stabbed at him. Berengar shrieked hysterically, ran from the room in a panic and up the tower stairs, with the ghostly image hurtling after him.

He was last seen alive screaming on the roof of the tower, by a guard standing below who'd been roused by the noise. The guard saw Berengar enveloped in a shining glow just before he tumbled to his death. When the guard rushed to him, he found Berengar's dagger, which was supposedly locked away, embedded in his heart.

After that, Berengar's men deserted Durance Guarde. No one would live there. Those who ven-

tured into the castle ended up dead, including a
wandering minstrel upon whom a stone from the
wall fell. Berengar's son Odo tried to pull the castle down. But when the men sent to do the job
tried to destroy the tower where Rowena died,
they all suddenly fell ill of the plague. No one tried
to complete the destruction of Durance Guard
ever again.

Galen scowled at the moon as he remembered
how long ago poor Rowena had died. Over two
hundred years had passed. There were fewer noblemen like Berengar in the kingdom, and a new
age of discovery was dawning over the world.
Since its abandonment a dense and gloomy forest
had grown up around the remnants of the once
mighty castle. But its evil reputation lived on in
legend and tales told around kitchen fires in villages at night. The local people thought that the
ghost of Lady Rowena still haunted the deserted
and crumbling towers, ready to pounce on unwary
visitors.

Galen sighed and went back to bed. Mayhap he
was being presumptuous. There might indeed be
unsettled business here. What did he know of the
power of a spirit, the spirit of a lady whose life had
been cut short by horror?

"No," he said as he crawled back into bed, "I've
seen no ghosts, no eerie lights or glowing shades."

Durance Guarde was simply an old fortress, de-
caying and shrouded with vines, crumbling to dust
with each passing year. The place was deserted and

dull, and these were the very reasons he'd been drawn to it in the first place.

LATER THAT MORNING Honor Jennings rode at the head of a retinue crossing de Marlowe land on its way to her father's home, Castle Stafford. Her pale face was surrounded by the traditional widow's barb. The white linen that covered her hair fit close to her chin, from which it fell in vertical pleats. In addition, she wore a white veil over the barb and a black one over that. Her gown, mantle, and boots were all black. On the third finger of her right hand she wore the plain gold ring of the Order of Vowesses.

Vowesses, as widows, pledged to remain single and celibate until death, although they retained the freedom and privileges of a married woman. Honor had been a widow for over four years. Married to Aymer Jennings when she was fourteen, she had few good memories of their time together. The match had been arranged, and Aymer had never bothered to hide his disappointment that his bride had turned out to be a rather plain creature with outlandish copper hair and a habit of tripping over her own gown.

A few months after they'd married, Aymer had consoled himself by leaving Honor at home while he went to court to advance the fortunes of his family. His accidental death had been a shock to his wife, but had not grieved his younger brother or the rest of his family. Ever mindful of Honor's rich dower rights, they hadn't been in a hurry to rid themselves of Aymer's widow.

By her remaining unattached, they could control the wealth she'd brought to the family as well as the dower rights. Honor had been happy to go her own way, allowing the Jennings to think what they wished. She refused all suitors, which pleased her relatives. Months passed into years in this nebulous manner, but recently the Jennings heir, Isidore, became alarmed at the attentions paid to her by several extremely persistent noblemen. He decided to assure himself of Honor's wealth by marrying her to an impecunious Jennings relative. Honor had refused to comply with his plan. Isidore insisted to the point that Honor became fearful that he would resort to force. So she had become a vowess instead.

Honor moved her chin back and forth, then scratched beneath the barb. It had itched since this morning when she'd donned it and the widow's weeds for the ceremony at which she took her vows. Absently she rubbed her mare's neck, then fidgeted with the two veils, leaving a streak of dirt on the white one. She hadn't yet noticed the hole she'd torn in the hem of her gown when she'd mounted.

At the moment, she was glancing covertly at one of the two noblemen who escorted her. On her right, Sir Lionel Titchwell was scowling at one of her men-at-arms. Like half a dozen others, he'd been furious at the news that—after four years of widowhood—she was to become a vowess rather than remarry. He coveted Castle Stafford and her inheritance. Since Sir Lionel wasn't above abducting her and forcing a marriage, Honor had demanded a large escort, much begrudged by her brother-in-law. To sweeten the incentive, Honor had promised to go home a week early, and Isidore had finally assigned an escort.

Lord Isidore had inherited his brother Aymer's lands and title after Aymer died childless. One snowy winter day while Aymer and Honor were visiting Castle Stafford, he'd gone riding along the river Eske a few miles from the castle. When Aymer failed to return, Sir Walter and his steward, Baldwin Trune, had taken a search party to look for him. Eventually they found a steep, muddy bank upon which they could see signs that Aymer's horse had lost his footing. Baldwin discovered a piece of Aymer's tunic caught on a half-submerged rock.

For days they searched the river, dragging it for miles in either direction, to no avail. When Aymer failed to appear after many months, he was declared dead, and Honor had been left alone among her husband's indifferent, avaricious relatives. Honor had always suspected Isidore would have married her himself in spite of the church's objections to men marrying their dead brothers' wives, but he already had a wife. At the very least, he wanted her dower lands. So she made a bargain with him. He could have the lands, and she would become a vowess and go home.

Upon hearing this proposal, Isidore finally realized Honor wasn't ever going to comply with his plans for her hand or her fortune. By then he would have sent an army with her to get her off Jennings property and reclaim those lands. It had been a price willingly paid, for Honor was not happy to remain near Isidore, who was openly hostile to her and now considered her a burden. Yes, it had been a wise bargain.

"And I'm right well content with my decision," Honor said to herself.

"My lady?" the man to her left said.

"Oh, naught but daydreams, my lord." Honor inclined her head politely at Lord Andrew Swan, her other persistent suitor.

Lord Andrew had spent the two days since they'd set out casting calculating glances, not at the men-at-arms, but at the silver bosses on the saddles and reins of the knights, at the chests of plate, jewels, and clothing and at the carts of furniture. He was a wealthy man, but always felt poor unless he was increasing his riches. Neither he nor Sir Lionel had more than glanced at Honor before making offers for her hand.

"By my troth, Lady Honor," said Lord Andrew, "I cannot believe you've become a vowess, and I'm sorely vexed thereby."

"I'm sure you don't mean to be blasphemous," Honor said gently.

Lord Andrew reddened and crossed himself. "Blessed be God, I do not."

Honor gave him a beatific smile that brightened to ecstasy. "Look you, my lords. That giant hawthorn marks the boundary between the Stafford and de Marlowe lands. I'm home!" She reined in her mare and bowed in the saddle. "This is where we part, and I thank you both most heartily for your care of me."

Sir Lionel narrowed his eyes. "I see no escort from your father. Mayhap we should remain until Sir Walter's men appear."

"Oh, there's no need," Honor said hastily. She gestured toward the four knights who formed the vanguard of their procession. "Lord Isidore's men will do that, but I pray you accept my deepest gratitude for your chivalry."

Chewing his lip in frustration, Sir Lionel bowed and pulled his horse out of line. Lord Andrew dragged his eyes from the wagon that carried Honor's waiting woman, her cook, and a casket of jewels. He saluted his would-be bride and without a farewell trotted after Sir Lionel. Honor waited until they were out of sight before she dismounted and led her horse off the road to stand beneath the ancient hawthorn. A few moments later Isidore's chief knight joined her.

Honor nodded to him. "God assoil your soul, good Sir Frederic. We've reached my father's demesne, and I shall await his men here. You may begin your journey home at once."

"Impossible, my lady."

"I pray you, good sir, don't dispute with me. Look." Honor pointed to a line of mounted men crossing a stream that wandered down from a line of forest-covered hills. "My escort is here, so there's little need to tarry."

"I must—"

"No, you mustn't." Honor took off her gloves and flapped them at the man. "Go away! I'm done with Jennings affairs and Jennings men. Oh, now you've made me lose my temper, may God forgive me. And I've only just taken my vows."

"Forgive me, lady. I didn't mean to."

"Then save me from a more grievous transgression and go away, Sir Frederic."

The knight hesitated.

Honor rolled her eyes. "I can vouchsafe that my father's men will be here before you're out of sight."

"Very well." Sir Frederic took her hand and kissed it. "May God protect you, good lady."

"And you, good sir."

The Jennings escort separated from Honor's retinue and went slowly down the path. Sir Frederic paused at a turn and watched until the Stafford banner appeared through the trees. Honor waved her gloves at him. He kicked his destrier into a trot, and he and his men disappeared. Honor counted to one hundred. Down the road her father's men approached.

"Ninety-nine, one hundred."

Gripping her veils, Honor tore them from her head. She ripped the barb off and flung it away. A cheer erupted from her lips as it flew into the limbs of the hawthorn. Whirling around, she danced in front of her mare, who backed away from her with pricked ears. Honor laughed and twirled around. Her hair came loose from the net confining it, and it tumbled in copper waves down her shoulders. As she danced, her waiting woman scrambled down from her wagon and hurried over to her.

"Jacoba, I'm free," Honor said. "I'm free!"

"I marvel they didn't see through your disguisings, I do." Jacoba crossed her arms and beamed at her mistress. Taller than most men, she was a woman of middle years whose chief concerns were finding a dye mixture that would cover the gray in her hair and trying to keep her mistress out of trouble.

Honor laughed, and soon she was surrounded by her servants—Dagobert the page, Father Theodoric the clerk, and Wilfred the groom.

Theodoric frowned and scratched under his cap. He was a former soldier and even after fifteen years as a cleric and secretary had yet to shed his warlike temperament. He was constantly trying to cultivate a virtuous attitude to make up for his faults.

"If I may embolden myself, my lady. Taking vows and not keeping them . . ."

"Oh, I'm going to keep them," Honor said. She stopped capering and grew serious. "Did I not tell you privily that this was the only way we could avoid being packed off to some lord? Did any of you wish to call another Jennings, or Sir Lionel, master?"

They shook their heads violently.

"No, my lady," said Theodoric. "I'd have sinned grievously if that happened. I'd have been forced to lop off Sir Lionel's head, may God forgive me."

Jacoba poked him with her elbow. "I'd have put nightshade in his porridge."

"I pray you heartily," Honor said, "No more such talk. We're going home."

As the Stafford escort arrived, she gathered her reins and mounted with Dagobert's help. After a brief greeting, she guided her mare beside the destrier of her father's most trusted knight, Sir Renard Fitz Gilbert. The party set out again and rode for almost an hour along the de Marlowe border. It was still morning, but the sun had burned the dew from the grass. The farther they went the more narrow the road grew, until it became little more than a path. Finally, as it wound around the edge of the forest to her right, Honor reined in once more. She glanced at a nearby hill. Much taller than the rest, it was even more shrouded in brush, forest, and vegetation than the others.

"We will break our fast here, Sir Renard."

The servants busied themselves with meal preparations and the soldiers saw to the horses. Informing Sir Renard that she would stretch her legs while the meal was being prepared, Honor walked into the forest with Jacoba. Only the groom Wilfred went with them, to stand guard at a distance. He was one of those young men who never seemed to outgrow his youthful awkwardness, which possibly was due to the extreme length of his arms and legs. Jacoba often remarked that it was a miracle he was able to get them all moving in the same direction.

Honor took refuge behind thick bushes to attend to her private needs, and then rejoined her servants.

"Come," she said, and she plunged deeper into the forest, in the direction of the tall hill. She led them to a clearing from which they had a better view of the hill. "I can't see it."

"What's that, my lady?" asked Jacoba.

"Durance Guarde."

Wilfred swallowed hard and gaped at the hill. "God save us. Durance Guarde?"

Shading her eyes, Honor didn't reply. She craned her neck, but failed to locate even a part of the old ruin.

"I must have a look," she muttered to herself.

"You can't, my lady," Wilfred said. "No one goes up there. I've never been this close to it, and I've lived me whole life on Stafford demesne."

Jacoba wrung her apron. "We thought you'd given up the idea of building at Durance Guarde, me lady. It's an evil place, and ruin befalls those that venture near it."

"Then stay here. I'll be back in a trice."

"No!" Wilfred and Jacoba cried.

Honor turned slowly to face them and said, "No? Who is mistress here?"

They stared at her, neither speaking.

"Exactly," Honor said. "I'll be back before I'm missed. It isn't far."

Lifting her skirts, Honor set off. She left the clearing for the shade of the forest and soon heard footsteps behind her. Jacoba trotted up, with Wilfred close behind.

"Your father would skin me and lop off me head if I let you go alone, my lady," Wilfred said in a shaky voice.

"That's what I told him," Jacoba added.

"Very well, but I'll hear no whining or complaints. You mustn't believe silly stories told to frighten children."

"Told to frighten adults, by my troth," muttered Jacoba.

"We'll be carried off by demons," Wilfred whispered, his eyes protruding from his skull.

"Nonsense," Honor said. She picked up her skirts once more and hopped over a lichen-encrusted log. The hem of her gown dragged and picked up bits of moss. "You'll see. There's naught at Durance Guarde but ruined towers full of spiders and owls."

TWO

❧

HONOR WALKED QUICKLY through the forest, shoving her way through stands of bushes, and vines that hung from tree limbs in great cascades. The closer she got to Durance Guarde, the denser the vegetation grew, and the trees seemed to get larger too. As she tramped on ferns and climbed over rocks and hillocks, she thought of the wonderful plans she had for this place.

She was going to build a manor house.

It wasn't to be an ordinary manor house, however. She was going fill it with wondrous things. She had ordered one of those marvelous contraptions from Germany—a printer's press. It came with slender metal rods called type, with a letter of the alphabet on each, and these little types could be arranged to make words. When the press arrived, a man would come with it who would teach her how to print a whole page, then more pages, and how to bind them into a book.

Theodoric was skeptical, despite having seen the printed books in Honor's library. He said this printer's press was a passing amusement that wouldn't last long. Honor had retorted that Mr. Caxton was printing Chaucer's *Canterbury Tales*, and that selling copies of that book and the Bible would make him rich, and able to print even more books.

She would also invite men of learning from Florence, Venice, and Ferrara to her new house. One of her few pleasant memories of Aymer was when she'd accompanied him to Florence for the wedding of Lorenzo de Medici. She'd begged Aymer to take her and eventually he had agreed. Honor was certain it had been because he hadn't wanted to hear her complaints if he refused. Besides, he could ignore her in Italy as well as he could in England.

Theirs had been a marriage arranged by their parents, and at first it had seemed an ideal alliance. The Jennings were ambitious and clever, but as a relatively new family, they needed the legitimacy a Stafford bride could provide. Honor's inheritance, while not immense, had been sufficient to tempt them to form an alliance. Rising in the world consumed Aymer Jennings' entire being. He spent half his time trying to cover his family's humble beginnings as peasant farmers and the other half weaseling his way into the favor of magnates who could help him. Honor later learned that this obsession with improving one's rank and wealth was a family trait, like long noses and feet that pointed inward. It was what compelled Aymer to falsify birth records in his home county to erase the low origins of his great-grandparents.

Barely fourteen, Honor had been like most girls of her station. She learned the skills a noble-woman would need to run her husband's manors, lands, and castles. But she'd also spent a great deal of her time reading tales of King Arthur, and about chivalrous knights and fair maidens. She had further peopled her imagination with the lovers made famous in minstrels' songs. When Honor's and Aymer's parents first introduced them shortly be-fore the betrothal, Aymer had seemed a perfect, gentle knight worthy of his own song. She hadn't been married a week before the truth smacked her in the face. It came when she stumbled upon Aymer in a stall in the stables, naked on top of a laundry maid.

Her illusions about Aymer vanished in an in-stant, and in the months that followed, she came to know him all too well. He didn't care whether his conduct hurt her. He expected her to carry out her wifely duties and refrain from interfering in his life. But mostly, he didn't think of her at all. She was just another person around the place, like his manservant or the horses in the stable. He simply didn't want to be bothered with her.

However, when it came to the trip to Italy, Honor had been determined not to be forgotten. She pestered him in person and in letters to take her along. For once, Aymer bowed to her wishes, and she was allowed to accompany him so long as she understood that he wouldn't have time to spend with her. So, while Aymer pursued his own business and pleasures in Italy, she met scholars engaged in studies of ancient Greece and Rome, who read Virgil, Plato, and Aristotle, and who were rediscovering the wonders of the ancient world. Once she'd experienced the excitement of this new learning, she didn't want to give it up when she went home. Just as exciting was her idea of inviting artists to visit and giving them commissions. She would fill her new house with paintings by Botticelli, Gozzoli, and Mantegna, and sculptures by Verrocchio.

Of course, all this would require funds, but she'd learned a few things from Lorenzo de Medici. Since Aymer was preoccupied with an Italian mistress, Honor learned about the new business practices the Italians had thought up—partnership agreements, holding companies, marine insurance, and credit transfers. She kept busy in Italy, because the more occupied she became, the less hurt she felt from being ignored by her husband-in-name-only. Now, as a widow and a vowess, she would be able to join the de Medici family in a partnership that would take wool from her estates to the Netherlands, then to France and Italy. Eventually fine wool and silk fabrics would return to her, and she would sell them, thus making the profits she needed to support her true interests.

Her occupations had been a delight and a comfort, because when she was engrossed in the study of painting or reading a contract, she wasn't dwelling on her many faults. For she knew that had she been more charming and comely, Aymer would have loved her. Honor could list her faults, and often did. She had a disfiguring spray of freckles across her nose and cheeks. She went around with smudges on her face and hands, and she usually had a tear or two in her gown. She was apt to spill things, drop things, or fall over them because she was thinking about her many projects. And she had interests no one else seemed to share.

In truth, most people thought her odd when they learned she was reading Plato or wanted to actually print books herself. No, she could understand why Aymer hadn't found her pleasing. That was why, when she'd first discovered his indifference, she'd tried so hard to change. She had tried be a lady worthy of courtly love, like the ones about whom the minstrels composed songs. Her attempts had ended in failure.

A sudden rush of wind recalled Honor to the present. She hadn't been walking long, but she'd left Wilfred and Jacoba behind. She could hear them stumbling through the bushes behind her. She turned to face the wind. Looking up she saw a line of thunderclouds boiling up in the distance and racing toward Durance Guarde. Through wildly waving tree branches she glimpsed a round tower. Half of it was gone, and it was covered with vines and clinging plants, but it was still recognizable.

"Lady Honor!"

"I'm here, Jacoba. Keep walking in the same direction and you'll come to the castle walls. I'm going on ahead."

Disregarding Jacoba's pleas that she wait, Honor clambered up the side of the hill. She pulled herself along using saplings and ended up beneath the high arch of the barbican of Durance Guarde. Two drum towers flanked the gate, but the wooden door that once sealed it was missing. Behind the barbican stood another gatehouse. Massive walls extended outward in either direction, but large portions of them lacked wall walks due to someone's deliberate destruction. There were several gaps where the wall had collapsed. Trees had grown up against enormous drum towers and brambles had implanted themselves on top of the crumbling walls.

Out of breath from her climb, Honor rested for a moment beneath the arch of the barbican. The wind was howling now, and several oak trees danced against the towers, their branches scraping against stone. As she watched a black mountain of a cloud soared into view, the sun vanished and the temperature dropped. Honor settled her mantle around her shoulders and hurried through the barbican. She would have to make haste if she was to

reach the keep, inspect it, and return to Sir
Renard before the rain began.

On the other side of the barbican there was a
deep ditch and remnants of a burned drawbridge.
At some time it had been repaired with old planks
from the ruins, but it looked undependable. Honor
heard a yelp. Glancing over her shoulder, she saw
Wilfred sprawled on his back in a nest of brambles
and vines. Jacoba was fussing at him and trying to
untangle his arms and legs from the creepers. If
Honor had been superstitious she would have said
Durance Guarde was trying to keep them out.

"You may remain here if you wish," Honor
called to them. "I won't be long."

Without waiting for an answer she scaled down
the ditch, but when she hauled herself up the last
yard or so, she stepped on her skirt and fell flat on
her face, feeling a seam rip at her waist. Sighing,
she got to her feet and dusted her hands on her
gown.

Massive and tree-shrouded, the keep of Durance
Guarde loomed before her. Round towers guarded
to the corners of the square keep. Their conical
roofs now had dozens of holes and served as perches
and nests for ravens.

Pausing at the base of the keep, Honor leaned
against the wind and peered up at the four towers
that guarded its corners. At intervals blank windows and arrow slits gaped open, black and omi-
nous. A shiver passed over her, and sheet lightning
flickered from a thunderhead behind the keep.

Honor felt a few windblown raindrops against her face and plunged on, over a spray of stones that had fallen from a wall and up a rickety wooden stair that led to a door set high in the keep. Odd how so many stone walls had collapsed, but the wooden staircase had survived.

She reached the door, which had no lock or bar. Blackened, reinforced with iron fittings, it seemed aged, but still serviceable. She pushed it, but it was stuck on rusted hinges. Behind her she heard Wilfred call out, but she continued to push against the door. What could be preventing it from opening? Honor looked up at the sky. Seeing the black clouds, she again realized that she didn't have much time. She backed up as far as she could on the landing, inhaled and ran at the door, intending to ram it with her shoulder.

At the last moment the door moved. Unable to stop, she crashed against it, and it flew back. Honor heard a sharp cry as the wood banged against something and she soared into the keep. Her foot caught on an obstacle, and she fell, but instead of hitting a stone floor, she landed on something not quite so hard.

Honor cried out in surprise. She lifted her head, brushed aside long copper tresses and found herself perched on top of a black shadow. Hard muscles surged beneath her, and she heard panting. Fear surged through her as the black figure growled. What had she disturbed in this crag of a place?

Suddenly the muscles beneath her swelled and quivered, and a hollow voice boomed into the darkness of the void beyond the door. "By the devil!"

In an instant Honor was tossed aside. She landed on her back staring up at a towering menace, and scrambled to get away from it. Blessed Trinity! She had fallen right on top of some demon. Her heart pounding, she scrambled to her feet as the demon approached. It passed into the dim light coming through the doorway, and Honor beheld a man dressed in black.

Her fear ebbed somewhat. This was no demon, at least not one she'd seen in books. Demons were ugly, and this man was beautiful, although at the moment he was grimacing with the effort to hide some physical agony.

Dazed, Honor could only stare at him. Sunburnished brown hair fell to his shoulders, and dark eyebrows accented startling eyes that reminded her of brown onyx glistening in sunlight. Fascinated and distracted by his physical beauty, Honor studied a wide expanse of chest, which tapered to a slim waist belted and laden with a dagger in a sheath. Honor's gaze drifted down the length of a leg the thickness of two of hers. Then she jumped as the man winced and sucked in his breath.

"By the devil," he repeated, touching a lump reddening on his forehead. He made a hissing sound. "You've cracked my skull." Honor backed away when he suddenly advanced a step and raised his voice. "Who are you?"

Honor halted and blinked at him. "Who are you?"

"You're the trespasser, it's for you to identify yourself."

"I am no trespasser," she said. "You're the trespasser. This is my land, and my castle, such as it is."

"By my troth, it is not."

"It is!" Honor narrowed her eyes and looked at the interloper more closely. "Here, now. I think I remember you. You're one of those de Marlowes."

She said the name as if it were a curse, for the de Marlowe brothers had teased her mercilessly when she was growing up. From perches high in the treetops, they would throw acorns at her when she passed by. They tried to frighten her with stories of ghosts and demons. Once they'd even stuck her on the well bucket at Castle Stafford, lowered her into the slimy darkness and left her there. She'd cried and screamed for help for what seemed like centuries before a scullion had passed by and rescued her. All the de Marlowes were evil, and she detested them.

"Yes," he said. "I'm a de Marlowe, now tell me who you are and get off my land."

Honor gritted her teeth and repeated slowly, "This is not your land."

"The devil take you. It is, and—why am I arguing with a fiery-haired little shrew?"

De Marlowe came toward her, and with each

step he seemed to grow ten feet. By the time he'd backed Honor to the wall beside the doorway, her head was bent back at an awkward angle, and her heart was pounding again. He stopped so close she could feel his warmth. Honor stared up into dark, burning eyes and tried not to show her uneasiness.

"Now that you know who I am, you're afraid, aren't you?" He leaned close and whispered in her ear. "This is a place of sorcery and black magic. Fell creatures inhabit Durance Guarde—the ravens, the spirits, and the shades. . . ." A crash of thunder made Honor cry out. De Marlowe smiled. "And me."

There was something about that smile that was more frightening than the thunder. Lightning struck somewhere close, and Honor bolted. Outside, Jacoba and Wilfred hovered in fear some distance from the keep. She rushed to the wooden landing and down the stairs, not daring to look behind her until she reached the ground. Then she turned and saw her tormentor leaning in the doorway, a black cloak swirling around his lean body. He gave her a mocking smile, undisturbed by the violent storm that raged around him. She remembered that mocking smile.

"Galen de Marlowe!" she cried.

His smile vanished. Grim, menacing, he left the doorway and headed down the stairs.

"My lady, run!"

For once Honor heeded Jacoba's advice. Lifting her skirts, she turned and raced across the ward past her servants as thunder and Galen de Marlowe's laughter chased after her. She didn't stop until she'd clambered across the ditch, through the barbican, and down the hill. Rain pelted her as she scrambled through the forest. Once, in the darkness of the storm, she mistook a thick sapling for de Marlowe and screamed. When she recognized the tree, she stood there staring at it until Wilfred and Jacoba caught up with her.

"I told you, lady," Wilfred said breathlessly. "Now you've gone and disturbed a sorcerer."

"That was no sorcerer," Honor said, her teeth chattering. "That was a false, black-hearted wretch named Galen de Marlowe."

"I was right!" Wilfred squeaked. "A sorcerer."

"Oh, my lady," Jacoba said as she wiped rain from her face, "you don't want to have anything to do with them de Marlowes."

Honor tugged at her skirt, which was sodden and clung to her legs, threatening to trip her. "Oh, I'm going to have much to do with him. Galen de Marlowe is a malicious, cunning knave, and he's not going to steal my land."

"But, my lady—"

Honor set out again, tramping through mud and puddles. "He thinks he can send me quavering and mewling from my own land. Mayhap he did this time, but I was unprepared. I'll teach him to go in fear and dread intolerable, and when I'm finished, he'll curse the day he set foot in Durance Guarde."

THREE

CASTLE STAFFORD WAS not as large as the fortresses built by old King Edward I to control the rebellious Welsh, but it had two concentric rings of defensive walls, a few mighty drum towers and a barbican, and it was only a little over a hundred years old. Visitors who first saw it would marvel at its beauty, for it was pristine white and seemed to float in a blue moat that more resembled a lake than a narrow stream. Being a newer structure, the castle lacked a keep. Instead, it boasted a great hall with glass windows, a solar, and guest chambers.

Oblivious to the beauty of her home, Honor Jennings tramped into the great hall without a glance at the windows that allowed sunlight to illuminate her soaked hair and gown. Shivering, she hurried to the fireplace and held her hands out to its warmth. Looking over her shoulder, she saw Jacoba carrying a jewel casket. The waiting woman sneezed, and Honor felt guilty for getting Jacoba caught in the rain.

Honor realized she was staring with apprehension at the double doors that had been left open for the new arrivals. "Curse it."

She turned her back to the fire and began to wring her hair. Ever since she had escaped Durance Guarde she'd been looking over her shoulder expecting to see Galen de Marlowe riding after her, black cape flying, on some hellish black stallion.

"Lackwit," she muttered. "It was only Galen de Marlowe, old Leekshanks."

De Marlowe was nine years older than she, but when she'd been five he'd annoyed her at a feast by refusing to allow her to ride his palfrey, and she'd retaliated. Pointing to his long, slim legs, she'd cried, "You look right silly on that horse with those terrible long legs. They're like leeks, skinny old leeks. Leekshanks, Leekshanks!"

He had ignored her, but his younger brothers had been nearby, heard her and took up the cry. She had been delighted with the scuffle that resulted. How many brothers were there? There was Simon, the next in age to Galen, who was the oldest. Then there were Macaire and the twins, Fulk and Fabron. Thanks be to God none of them seemed to have taken up residence with Galen on

"Oh, excellent. Yes, so it did. It will do the crops and trees much good. Welcome home, child." Sir Walter strode to her and kissed her forehead. "Now, Perkin, about the quinces."

"Father," Honor said with a groan. "Forget the quinces and tell me why you allowed Galen de Marlowe to claim Durance Guarde."

"Who? I allowed no one to claim Durance Guarde. There must be some mistake." Sir Walter looked down at his map. "I wonder if I could plant—"

"Father!"

"What, child?"

"I want to build a house at Durance Guarde, and Galen de Marlowe has decided to live there."

"Then build it somewhere else."

"Father, he tossed me out. Are you going to allow him to insult me? You should make him give it up."

Sir Walter folded his map and shook his head. "I'll not cross swords with a man who calls King Edward friend. The only way to survive the contendings between the houses of Lancaster and York is to stay out of them and keep the good graces of the current king. If de Marlowe wants that old ruin, let him have it."

"But I want it." Honor eyed her father. "You don't believe those rumors about him, do you?"

Sir Walter's gaze strayed back to the folded map. "I've heard strange reports, child."

Perkin had been standing nearby awaiting his master, and he nodded vigorously. Honor's eyebrows met in the middle of her forehead.

"He's fostered evil rumors about himself apurpose."

"God save us, why?" Sir Walter asked.

"So that he can go unchallenged by any man." Honor sneezed. "I knew him when he was old Leekshanks."

"Be quiet, child. No more shrewish language regarding Lord Galen. It's not wise to make an enemy of so powerful a man. Why are you so evil disposed toward him?"

Honor blushed and pressed her lips together. "He chased me off my own land. Galen de Marlowe has no chivalry. He's a mean, conniving churl, and I hate him."

"You're being churlish yourself, my girl." Sir Walter staved off her response with a raised finger. "No. There's an end to the matter. Choose some other place to build your new house. Now, go put on some dry clothing, or by vespers you'll have an ague. Come Perkin, I want to talk about the medicinal herbs. I want to see the feverfew, the mouse-ear, and the pimpernel, and we must hurry because I've yet to ride today."

Honor scowled at her father, but quickly put on a smile when he suddenly turned back to her. "And tonight we'll talk about who you're going to marry. The king will soon want to know. Can't put it off now that you've done with the Jennings."

"But I'm a vowess."

"And if King Edward hears of it, he'll be furious and make you renounce your vows, so you might as well accustom yourself to giving them up. You know I only agreed to let you become a vowess temporarily, to help you rid yourself of the Jennings. Castle Stafford must have an heir, my child. You can't leave our people without someone to take care of them."

"I'm not. I'll take care of them."

"Of course you will. Now run upstairs and dry yourself. Then come find me and tell me who you want to marry."

"No one." At his severe look, she added, "No one at the moment, Father. I promise I'll think of suitors after I build my house at Durance Guarde."

"I'll make a list for you."

Honor threw up her hands as Sir Walter strode out of the hall, deep in conversation with Perkin. She'd hoped to convince Father that she wished to remain a widow. Widowhood provided a woman with independence. She could do as she liked with her property and govern her own life. As a married woman she'd be subject to a husband again.

No, she was better off without a man. Widowhood was the perfect state for her. If she could build her house at Durance Guarde, which was remote and deserted, the king might forget about her. Also, she could defend herself from there against any overzealous suitors who might attempt to force her into marriage.

She knew Father would harry her until she consented to marry again. But once she lived at Durance Guarde, he'd forget about her for long stretches of time. Father loved her, but he easily became distracted by his orchards, by his horses, dogs, and falcons, and by his collection of books. If only her mother were here. Mother had died giving birth to a stillborn son not long after Honor married, and Honor still considered sometimes, with a touch of self-pity, how different her life would have been had her mother lived.

A practical and headstrong woman, Jane Stafford would have understood Honor's desire for independence. Honor still remembered how Mother would get her own way if she desired something and didn't wish to quarrel. Father hated buying new clothing. He hated picking out fabrics, standing still for fittings, and choosing his daily outfits. If Jane showed him new materials or garments, he'd refuse to purchase them despite needing them. So Jane simply ordered new cloaks, hose, robes, or tunics and gave them to Sir Walter as presents. Sir Walter, having forgotten the fabrics and garments completely, accepted them with delight.

Honor smiled at the memory as she lifted her heavy, wet skirts and plodded up the stairs to her chamber. "I won't have to lie, by my troth. I'll simply refrain from discussing the subject of suitors."

Sir Walter would be too busy to bother her much. The whole demesne was busy in spring.

Plowing, harrowing, and sowing had to be done, but along with these vital chores the peasants had to clear ditches, and repair broken banks, hedges, and fences. The manorial account rolls would swell with the costs of making and repairing tools, keeping animals, repairing mills and cowsheds, and paying mole catchers. In summer, the harvest would occupy him. If she was fortunate, she could avoid the unpleasant subject of remarriage until next winter. By that time she would have thought of new reasons to remain a vowess.

"Now," she whispered, "how to eject old Leekshanks from Durance Guarde. That is the question."

Jacoba was in Honor's chamber laying out dry clothing on the bed when Honor entered, deep in thought.

"Lady," Jacoba said, holding out a drying cloth.

Honor took it, wiped her face, and patted her hair. As Jacoba began to strip the layers of soaked clothing from her, Honor frowned.

"I'm foully vexed. How am I to get rid of that cursed invading knave?"

"Oh, lady, you're not still thinking of that, are you? If you test him, there'll be terrible assaults and affrays, and your father will be furious."

"I'm not going to attack him, Jacoba."

Honor struggled out of her wet shift and pulled on a dry one, then put on a white underdress and a plain black gown and belt. She sat on the bed while Jacoba combed the tangles out of her hair. Tapping her nail against her front teeth, she thought hard.

"Poison is too drastic."

"It's a sin," Jacoba said as she combed.

"That too," Honor replied. "If we make the roof leak in his chamber, he'll simply repair it."

"Can you bring suit, me lady?"

"Against a man who drinks with the king? I don't wish to call attention to myself and be forced to marry again. And anyway, a suit wouldn't frighten him. What frightens a warrior, Jacoba? What frightens a man who people think is a sorcerer?"

"Naught, lady."

Honor played with a strand of copper hair. "Think, Jacoba. What frightens a man who consorts with demons, devils, and spirits?" She nibbled the ends of her hair, then dropped them. "That's it!"

Jacoba started. "Lady Honor, you near stopped me heart."

"Leave my hair for a moment." She hurried to the door and called downstairs. "Theodoric, come here at once."

Honor swept across the chamber, opened a carved chest and took out a stack of used parchment she kept for note taking. Next came a quill, ink, and a blotter.

Theodoric entered. "Lady?"

"Come here and write as I speak. Hurry, before I

forget my ideas. Let me see, I'll need a white gown, and a long white wig. Write, Theodoric, write." She paced in front of the clerk while Jacoba looked on in confusion. "My face and skin have to be white too. Write this, Theodoric—ground alabaster, beeswax, ass's milk, oil of white poppies. And I'll need something to make the stuff reflect light—egg whites, a coating of egg whites."

She strode over to the small chest that contained her cosmetics and fumbled among the jars and bottles. "Write down kohl, and belladonna to make my pupils huge." She began pacing again. "And I'll need a screen of some kind. Cobweb lawn, the most transparent linen there is. Jacoba, you and Wilfred will accompany me to Holywell town. The market there is bound to have cobweb lawn."

"I know what you're planning, lady," said Theodoric, "and it won't work. Not after you had that terrible quarrel with him. He'll be expecting something."

"Wherefore I'll wait at least a fortnight," Honor replied. "Ah, Dagobert."

Her young page came in bearing her traveling altar and placed it on the bed. Unlike most pages, Dagobert wasn't the son of an aristocratic family, fostered out to a noble household; he was the son of an unmarried kitchen maid, Adela Trune, who had died in Aymer's employ. Adela had been the daughter of Sir Walter Stafford's steward, Baldwin. One day a few months before Aymer died, Adela and another woman were dumping a heavy load of grout into an enormous boiling vat at the brewhouse. She lost her footing and fell in. Servants dragged her out, but she died three days later. Dagobert was left an orphan at the age of four.

Against Aymer's wishes, Honor had taken the boy under her protection. Now Theodoric was teaching him to read and write. She'd never told anyone one of the most important reasons for her actions—she suspected that Aymer was Dagobert's father. Adela would never speak about the father, but her son had Aymer's jet-black hair and dusky rose lips, his stocky frame, and winning expression. What he lacked was Aymer's callousness. He was standing beside the bed, rocking on his heels and looking at her with his customary solemn adoration. Honor smiled at him and held out her hand. He burst into a smile, bounced over to her, and grabbed her hand. He bowed over it and planted a wet kiss.

"God save you, me lady." He was also getting lessons in deportment from Jacoba.

"I thank you heartily, Master Dagobert." Honor curtsied, laughed, and kissed his cheek.

Dagobert flushed and looked beleaguered. "Aw, me lady."

"Your pardon, Dagobert." She touched the tip of his nose with her forefinger. "Have you had your lesson today?"

"It's too late, me lady." Dagobert yawned elaborately. "I am brought right low and weak by this day's travels."

"Then you'll have two lessons tomorrow."

"Aw, me lady."

"But you may accompany me to Holywell market."

Dagobert grinned.

Honor took his hand again. "And while we're there, I want you to speak to as many of the folk at the market as you may. I want you to talk about something quite marvelous. Have you ever heard the tale of the lady Rowena and the castle of Durance Guarde?"

FOUR

In the forest of Durance Guarde gnarled
and disfigured trees cast long shadows of such
blackness that they seemed to consume what little
light filtered through the canopy. Dust motes
floated undisturbed in the late afternoon shafts of
light. Birds were scarce and silent, and foxes kept
to their dens. Overhead a hawk coasted on an up-
draft, but refrained from uttering its raucous cry.
The whole forest seemed to hold its breath. Below,
in the ward that surrounded the keep, Galen de
Marlowe listened to the silence as he dumped oats
into a bucket for his horse and left the dilapidated
stable.

Unaffected by the oppressive quiet of the forest,
Galen de Marlowe stepped into the sunshine and

inhaled the scent of wildflowers—primroses, laven-
der, and violets. He felt renewed, as if he'd slept
undisturbed for a month. How paradoxical that the
little shrew who'd nearly bashed a hole in his head
was responsible for this wondrous improvement.
The night after he'd chased her out of Durance
Guarde, he'd slept without being tormented by the
vision.

It made no sense, for on the morning she'd invaded the keep he'd felt exhausted from worry and
lack of rest. He'd slept late and had just come
downstairs from Berengar's Tower. He was about to
go outside, had his hand on the door, when it
sprang open and rammed him on the forehead. By
God's mercy, he still felt the pain of that blow.
He'd landed on his back, and the next thing he
knew, a creature with flaming hair and black
clothing was sitting on his chest, crushing him. He
remembered little of what she'd said—shouted—
at him. And then she'd tried to evict him from his
own land, by the Trinity.

At first he'd been so surprised he hadn't reacted.
Then he'd noticed her wondrous fiery hair. And
then he'd heard her witch's screech. It pierced his
skull and magnified the pain; it ruined his attempt
to preserve what was left of his composure, and
he'd turned on her. Perhaps he'd been harsh, but
he wasn't used to young women knocking him
over like that.

Galen walked over to the well and began to

lower the bucket. He'd finally remembered who the copper-haired shrew was—Honor Stafford. No, Lady Honor Jennings. Who would have thought that nuisance of a child would grow to be so pleasing to behold? And still be a nuisance as an adult. He would have pitied Aymer Jennings if he were still alive. As the thought of Jennings' death flitted through his head, Galen felt a surge of darkness, as if a vision were coming. Then it was gone.

Evidently she hasn't banished all visions, Galen thought. Lady Honor had worked a little magic, but not a miracle. Surely she hadn't come home for good. No, she'd be marrying again soon, and he hoped to some poor soul whose demesne was far to the north.

That was uncharitable. After all, she'd cured him of that menacing vision. He slept well now because of dreams that had replaced the vision. Dreams of Lady Honor. That first night he'd fallen asleep, weary from the pain in his head, and re-lived the encounter with the lady. Only this time when he drew close to frighten her into retreat, she hadn't run away. He touched those strands of copper hair and found bronze, gold, and even silver. He pressed against her, and sensation flooded his body. The sun invaded his veins and turned his blood to liquid fire.

The dream went on, wrapping tendrils of arousal around him, leading him on, deeper and deeper into captivation until he opened his eyes to a new day. Galen smiled, then realized he'd been standing in the middle of the ward with a bucket in his hand, grinning foolishly.

"Cease this folly," he said to himself. "Would you have it said you've been undone by a woman?"

He watered his horse and was returning the bucket to the well when his manservant stuck his head around the door of the keep with great reluctance. Ralph's hair was disappearing quickly, and he walked like a chicken, darting his head forward with each step. Galen had saved his life in battle, and Ralph went wherever Galen did. Unfortunately for Ralph, he'd acquired a taste for the small luxuries afforded a rich nobleman—and the nobleman's manservant—while Galen was indifferent to them.

"God save your lordship, but you'd better come inside."

Galen set the bucket down and put his fists on his hips. "For God's mercy, Ralph, I told you there's nothing to fear. The village folk are an ignorant lot and see apparitions and shades in every patch of mist and fog."

"It be Lady Rowena's shade they're seeing, lordship." Ralph peered around the keep, eyeing the long shadows cast by the abandoned towers. "Only two days hence Snel the goatherder saw her a weeping and moaning in Ditchley Vale. She was pale, and she—she glowed with supernatural light!"

"Snel the goatherd leaves milk in little wooden bowls on his doorstep for fairies to drink during the night."

Ralph goggled at him. "And they do?"

"No," Galen replied with irritation. "No, Ralph, they don't. If there are fairies, they've magic enough to get their own food. And there's no shade of Lady Rowena either."

He wasn't about to mention the strange sounds he'd heard a few nights ago. He'd been coming home from a long walk, and darkness had come early in the midst of the thick forest of Durance Guarde. He'd turned around a sharp bend in the path that led to the castle and encountered a wraithlike figure. It had been hanging in the air, obscured by saplings and the moss that hung from tree branches. He had taken a step toward it, and it vanished as suddenly as it had appeared. When he moved farther off the path, he realized he was seeing the glow of light from one of the castle windows. What an addlepate. He'd had real visions too many times to take fright at his own imaginings.

"Better come in before the sun goes down, lordship."

Sighing, Galen started toward the keep. "Go on. I'll watch the sun set before dinner. And this time mind those quail. I spent all morning trapping them, and I don't want them burned; I want them roasted."

"Er, then you'd better come to dinner now, lordship."

Galen followed Ralph inside and over to the circular fireplace that once served as the only heat in the great hall. A spit had been erected over a pile of burning logs, and Ralph was barely in time to keep the quail from turning black. In spite of the manservant's complaining Galen was glad of his company. He loved his brothers, but the four of them were difficult to manage all at once, and when they sensed trouble they descended upon him like vultures. Each was eager to help; each had a different opinion of what Galen should do about his problems, and only Fulk refrained from expressing it.

The de Marlowe gifts made them different from most aristocratic families. To survive they'd kept together, fostered to the household of a Welsh prince, a relative who knew their secret. Such closeness was unusual among the aristocracy. Look at the royal family. Brother would kill brother for the throne. Galen's brothers would give their lives for him. That was what he feared. Even knowing about this vision risked one's life, and he wanted to spare Simon, Macaire, Fulk, and Fabron.

Galen dragged his attention back to the meal. The balding crown of Ralph's head gleamed as he plopped quail onto a wooden tray, and they began to eat. That is, Galen ate and Ralph complained. Ralph was a city man.

"I miss the cookshops in London, I do. Never had better venison than at Eda's shop in Candlewick Street."

"Hmm."

"Makes a lovely cameline sauce, does Eda."

Ralph took another bite of his quail and winced. "Got a crick in me neck from that horrible pallet you make me sleep on, lordship. Back home I got a nice trundle bed with a lovely mattress stuffed with straw and goose down, and nice tansy to keep the fleas away. Here the fleas have had centuries to breed so they're thick as flies on a turd."

"Ralph, I'm eating."

"Sorry, lordship." Ralph took a long drink from a leather tankard and grimaced, revealing a gap where he'd lost a molar to decay. "No proper pottery, nor plate, nor glass for drinking from neither. I had to put polished horn in me window to keep out the drafts."

"Your life is a trial, Ralph."

"It is, lordship." The manservant brightened. "But I purchased a rice pudding in Holywell village. It's flavored with spices and honey and wine, just as you like it."

"You're a good man, Ralph."

"I'm sore tried, lordship." Ralph cast a sideways glance at his master and groaned. "Me back is a torment. I got bit by some poisonous worm yester e'en, and I swear this ale we get from Snel has lye in it. Me guts is raw. If we don't go back to London town soon, I'll perish in this savage place."

"We're staying here, Ralph."

The manservant fell silent. He uncovered a large wooden bowl and served the rice pudding. With his spoon halfway to his mouth he darted a look over his shoulder. Although a dozen candles had been placed around, the hall was so vast that most of it lay in darkness. The ceiling was vaulted and rose two stories high. A gallery ran around the second level, providing more darkness beyond its arches.

"Did you hear something, lordship?"

Galen didn't even look up from his pudding. "It was the wind."

"There be no wind today."

"It picks up as the sun goes down."

"Yester e'en I was on me way to the guarderobe in the middle of the night, and I looked out one of the arrow slits." Ralph lowered his voice. "I swear, lordship, I saw a flickery light in Rowena's Tower. By my faith, I did."

"You probably saw the light from my room reflected off the wall," Galen said. Rowena's Tower projected from Berengar's Tower, and from his chamber he could see the window of the room where the poor girl had been kept prisoner.

Ralph was shaking his head. "No, lordship. It was a strange shimmering glow." He lowered his voice and glanced around the hall again. "And I saw a shadow pass by her window."

Galen put down his bowl and spoon and regarded his manservant with exasperation.

"No more tales of shadows and shades, Ralph. I'm not going home, and I'm not going back to court. You'll have to do without luxuries for a while longer."

"Oh, lordship—"

"But I give you leave to improve this place and make yourself more comfortable."

Ralph looked only a bit more cheerful. "It will take a merchant's fortune to amend this ruin."

"Begin with your own chamber, then, and don't bother me."

"Yes, master." Ralph brightened. "I'll purchase a new bed. I'll order one in Holywell town upon the morrow."

"Good, then you won't be pestering me."

Galen rose and headed for the stairs that wound up Berengar's Tower. "You did well with the quail this time."

"And I'll hire a cook."

"No servants."

"But we need a cook, lordship."

"If you bring one soul into this keep, I'll make you go fishing for carp and clean the cursed things yourself."

Galen left the hall with the laments of his manservant echoing off the vaulted ceiling. He climbed the stairs then he reached a ladder and trap-door to the roof of Berengar's Tower and was in time to watch the sun sink below the treetops. As he'd told Ralph, the wind had picked up as the sunlight faded, and he breathed in the smell of forest—soil, dead leaves, grasses, and wildflowers. After a day spent hunting and riding across the countryside, he was bone-weary. He glanced in the direction of the Stafford lands. The castle was behind another line of hills, and he wondered again if

Lady Honor had gone there or back home to her dower lands.

Mayhap she would pass this way again. He wouldn't mind seeing her, as long as she refrained from claiming land his family had owned for countless generations. Galen felt a stir of desire and directed his thoughts elsewhere. He was tired, but he'd never get to sleep if he kept thinking about lying on the keep floor with ladies squirming around on top of him. He descended to his chamber and went to bed.

He didn't know how long he'd been asleep when he suddenly bolted upright and wide awake. His gaze darted around the chamber, but found nothing out of the ordinary. He waited, listening to his own breathing. His blood froze as a long hollow moan floated on the breeze through the open window. Galen rose, picked up his belt and sword, and went to the window.

Naked and shivering, he looked out at the irregular line of the wall walk, at the towers that marched around the outer wall, and saw nothing. The moan came again, a long keening noise like a damned soul. Gooseflesh rose on his skin, and a spike of alarm went through him. Never had he heard that noise before. It seemed to arise from the air itself, and it sounded as though something unearthly was in torment. Another wail penetrated his ears and reverberated in his skull. He sucked in his breath as it seemed to take forever to fade.

Then he saw it, a glow coming from Rowena's

Tower. His room was higher, and a great space separated him from the wall in which the window was placed, but he could see a pale, shimmering glow emanating from the room where Lady Rowena had been kept.

"Rowena?" he whispered.

Galen leaned out, to see more closely, and a white figure formed itself out of the light. For a moment he stopped breathing as the apparition took shape—a woman dressed in a diaphanous white gown with long trailing sleeves. Her skin was dead white, and it reflected the unearthly light that surrounded her. She lifted pale arms and held them out to him. Her mouth opened. It was a dark gaping hole in a pale face. Although her lips didn't move, that spectral wail issued forth, echoing off the walls of the castle and fading away on the wind.

Galen beheld the long, white-blonde hair, the pale skin. "Dear Lord, *Rowena.*"

Then reason reasserted itself. It couldn't be Rowena. Rowena had been dark-haired. He closed his eyes in pain, then opened them to find that shimmering white-blonde hair filling his vision. There was only one woman he'd ever known with that silvery blonde hair.

He trembled and stuttered the name of his dead wife. "Con . . . Constance?"

As Galen stared, the apparition seemed to grow smaller, and he realized she was leaving. In an instant the light and the woman vanished, and Rowena's Tower was dark once more.

Galen kept staring at the vacant window below him. "Constance?" Then he shook himself. It couldn't have been Constance. "By all the devils in hell!"

He tossed his sword on the bed, pulled on hose, tunic, and boots and belted on his sword. He raced out of his chamber, holding tinder and flint in shaking hands. Lighting a torch that was set in a wall sconce, he grabbed it and hurtled downstairs, through a passage and into Rowena's Tower. Breathing heavily, he took the stairs two at a time and stopped at the door to Rowena's chamber. He lifted the latch and shoved the door open. It swung back with a long, loud creak, but nothing came out of the chamber but chilly air.

His heart beating fast, his mind a sea of pain and trepidation at the thought of Constance, Galen held the torch high and peered inside. Nothing. He took a cautious step back and drew his sword. It encountered no obstacles. He searched the room, but found naught out of the ordinary. It was a large chamber with a fan-vaulted ceiling. Once there had been tiles on the floor, but they'd been looted, leaving only the bare wood. Galen carefully approached the window, holding his sword before him, and looked out. He could see part of the wall walk, but most of his view was blocked by the massive walls of Berengar's Tower.

He began to feel foolish. Constance was in heaven, and her pure soul had no cause to haunt this place. The apparition must have been in his mind. He sheathed his sword with a sigh of relief. He'd been listening to Ralph too long if he was even considering that he saw Rowena. He groaned aloud and left the chamber, heading for his own. Why would he have a vision of a poor girl dead some two centuries? Then a more sinister thought occurred to him. What if that shimmering glow he'd seen the other night on the path hadn't been light from the castle? That meant either he was seeing spirits, or he was going mad, or both. Mayhap the strain of the Tower vision had affected his reason. Then there was another possibility; these ghostly sightings of his could be part of another vision. His hands were shaking, and he broke into a cold sweat.

If this was another vision, he would go mad. He'd had enough. He could stand no more of them. He didn't want to see murdered children, bloody battlefields, or dead women.

Halfway up the stairs to his chamber he stopped, put the torch in a sconce, and leaned against the wall. Holy Trinity! Deliver him from this foul curse! He was weary of these visions that plagued him awake and in his sleep. It had cost him much, more than he wanted to remember. He slumped to the floor, his sword between his knees, and cooled his burning forehead in his palms, trying to banish the mistaken image of Constance from his mind.

Once he'd been young, happy and confident, able to stand against all that the world might hurl at him. He'd had a wife and two children, a girl and a boy. He'd been fond of his beautiful wife. If he hadn't loved her, neither of them knew it, for their parents had matched them young, and there had been no chance to miss love. Constance had been thirteen, and he'd been two years older when they married. The births of Gisela and Oliver had drawn them together, and they had worked as partners. Constance governed the children and his home, Argent.

Gisela loved horses, and Galen had feared for her safety since she was three and insisted on riding a pony. At nine years of age she rode a horse as fearlessly as he had at fifteen. Six-year-old Oliver preferred his gentle pony and kept the whole castle laughing with his jests and pranks.

On a cold day in February Galen had a vision of danger that threatened a friend and rode out in all haste to warn him. The journey took three days, and he returned to find that a Yorkist rival, Baron Roger Scrope, had attacked Argent while the gates were open and the drawbridge down to receive shipments of goods from London. Scrope, who coveted Argent and its rich fields and forests, had been as lawless and evil as old Berengar, but Galen had always beaten him in the few open fights they'd had. Now the castle was in flames. Scrope had cornered Constance, Gisela, and Oliver in the solar and skewered each with his own sword.

Near mad with grief and rage, Galen had

tracked Roger Scrope down, in the hunting lodge where he'd gone to weather the storm of outrage that had resulted from his raid. Galen and his men surrounded the lodge, allowed Scrope's servants to go free, and set fire to the place. When Scrope and his knights fled, a hail of arrows from longbows rained down on them. Galen found Scrope hiding in the stables, forced him into the kitchen yard, and attacked. Scrope's venality was no match for Galen's cold rage. He ended up begging piteously for his life. At least, Galen assumed that was what he was crying as he ran his sword through Scrope's throat and pinned him to the ground. Galen watched him die, feeling nothing, and wishing that he could die too.

In the stairwell of Berengar's Tower Galen made a strangled sound in his throat and fought back tears. That had been seven years ago. The pain would never go away, and neither would the knowledge that if had he not left to follow one of his visions, Constance, Gisela, and Oliver would still be alive.

He wasn't going to sleep tonight. Galen picked up the torch and wandered aimlessly around the keep. Eventually he ended up back in Rowena's chamber. He slumped on the bench and looked out the window at the expanse of bare rock that was Berengar's Tower. Tired of holding the torch, he propped it in a sconce. Then he turned around, leaned against the scarred window embrasure and stared at the floor, wretched. His boot slid over the floorboards as he leaned forward and rested his forearms on his knees and closed his eyes. They opened again, and he bent down. Abruptly he picked up the torch and held it close to the floor.

In the dust left from centuries of neglect he saw what he should not have been able to see—footprints. Someone had been here. Someone real. Galen walked around the trail of prints, studying them. A real person had been in this chamber. Who?

He knelt down and studied the imprints. They were small, light footprints. Had mischievous children played a prank on him? Galen rubbed his chin, then narrowed his eyes. These weren't children's footprints. They were the prints of a woman's slipper.

And drops of candle wax. That's what his boot had slid over so easily. Dried wax. Ghosts didn't leave footprints, nor did they need candles.

Galen touched the bits of wax, then straightened and contemplated the footprints. Children wouldn't come to Durance Guarde at night. Few dared to come near it at any time. In truth, there was only one person he'd encountered since he'd been here who might dare to go into Rowena's Tower at night. Only one who wore a small slipper. Only one who might be crazed enough to pose as a ghost.

Lady Honor the shrew, by God's mercy.

FIVE

ER FACE PLASTERED with a sickly white paint, Honor crept onto the landing outside Rowena's chamber and pushed open the door. She clutched a bundle that contained her wig and spare jar of alabaster paste. Jacoba stood nearby holding a small candle. Wilfred and Theodoric followed Honor inside bearing larger parcels.

Wilfred pulled tall, fat candles and two torches from his bundle, while Jacoba produced a piece of dark wool fabric, a length of white cobweb lawn, and two short wooden wands. Theodoric set his bundle down with a *clank*, which made the others jump.

"God save us!" Honor hissed. "I told you to be careful."

"Sorry, me lady," Theodoric said. He pulled a

length of chain and a small copper cooking pot from his bundle and left to continue upstairs to the roof.

Holding the dark fabric, Wilfred jumped onto the stone bench below the window and held it across the window. His hands shook, and he muttered prayers while Jacoba inspected Honor's face paint.

"It's still good, lady."

"Then light the candles and torches."

Honor threw off her cloak to reveal an old-fashioned gown of thin, white wool. It was long and full-skirted, with wide sleeves that revealed tight undersleeves. She wore a silver girdle low on her hips. Jacoba brought her the horsehair wig, one she'd had made and dyed in secret at Castle Stafford. The hem and long oversleeves of the gown had been cut in slits so that when Honor moved the ragged edges trailed and floated.

Donning the wig, Honor climbed up beside Wilfred on the bench. After Jacoba lit the remaining candles that had been placed on either side of the bench, she lighted the torches and picked up the cobweb lawn. She had tied the corners of the lawn to the two wands, and handed one to Wilfred, who was still holding the dark screen over the window.

Once Jacoba was in place opposite him, he dropped the screen, and together they waved the rods slowly, cobweb lawn rippling between them. The moment the screen dropped, Honor swayed and held out her arms. She heard Theodoric wailing into the cooking pot on the roof. She opened her mouth and put her hands near her face as if she were weeping, but she was careful not to touch the plaster on her cheeks.

They had rehearsed this scene many times over the last few weeks, and the whole demesne was alive with talk of Rowena's ghost. Four days earlier they'd played their haunting scene near Durance Guarde for the first time. She'd stood on a hillock with her companions behind her holding candles and in front of her waving the cloth. Galen had come down the path to the castle, stopped and stared at her. He'd looked as if someone had kicked him in the stomach, but she must not have remained on the hillock long enough, for he'd recovered himself and gone on as if nothing had happened. That's when she had decided to haunt the castle itself.

The moment she saw movement at the window in Berengar's Tower, she would hear Theodoric's wails grow louder. That was the signal. He would wait only two more wails before hurrying downstairs. She would back away from the window, then crouch and douse all the lights. Then they would throw everything into the sacks and run. If Galen de Marlowe didn't leave after tonight, she would have to haunt another tower farther away, because the cursed man had chased them instead of cowering in fright like he was supposed to do. Last time they'd barely gotten out of the keep in time.

Honor swept her arms up and swayed some more. She had to stop herself from grinning when she remembered the way de Marlowe had leaned out his window the first time he'd seen her inside the tower. She wished she'd been able to see him clearly, but of course it had been too dark for that. What a sight he must have been gawping at her in fear. Surely this would be the last time she'd have to perform this farce.

She dearly wanted this ruse to succeed. She needed her new manor house, her new life. Without her plans and schemes for the improvement of life, like the printer's press, she felt empty. But she could do something helpful, make up for her failure as a wife. She had so much to give, if only Galen de Marlowe would get out of her way and let her get on with it.

Theodoric's wailing suddenly rose, then ended on a shriek. Honor's arms froze, and she peered across the emptiness of the night to Berengar's Tower. De Marlowe wasn't at his window, but something on the roof caught her eye, and she nearly cried out. A sickly greenish-white glow rose from the tower, and something horrible rose up from it. Honor heard Wilfred and Jacoba gasp as a giant black creature took form. It seemed to be wearing a cassocklike garment with a hood, but there was nothing inside that hood. No eyes, no mouth, no face at all.

Suddenly the creature raised its arms, and long,

skeletal limbs ending in bony hands appeared. It pointed straight at Honor and uttered an inhuman screech.

"God's mercy!" Honor took a step back and nearly fell off the bench. Wilfred and Jacoba dropped the cobweb lawn and grabbed her. They jumped to the floor.

Theodoric clattered down the stairs, passed the door and cried, "Run, lady, run for your life!"

Wilfred and Jacoba stood motionless and shaking.

Honor shoved them toward the door. "Run!"

They burst into a gallop, caught up with Theodoric, and scrambled through a passage that led to the keep stairs and hurtled down them to the hall. They ran across the hall, with Honor in front. She hauled the door open to find another black monster behind it. Honor screamed and drew back, bumping into Wilfred, who crossed himself and mumbled feverish prayers. Theodoric held up the cross he wore on a chain around his neck, his mouth working silently. Jacoba clung to Honor's arm and whimpered. They kept retreating as a group when the black figure stepped over the threshold.

Her eyes fixed on the creature, Honor trembled as they neared the dying light of the fire in the center of the hall. The figure moved into the light and shoved back the hood of its cloak. Galen de Marlowe regarded them calmly.

"Ah, uninvited guests." He rested his hand on the hilt of his sheathed sword. "Leaving so quickly?"

Honor tried to speak, but all that came out was a squeak. Wilfred was still babbling, but he pointed in the direction of Berengar's Tower. De Marlowe glanced that way.

"Oh. You've met him."

Honor found her voice. "Wh-who?"

"Why, old Berengar, of course. You must have disturbed him with all that noise."

De Marlowe moved so suddenly that he was upon her before she could get away. He grasped one of her sleeves to hold her still. His voice rang in her ears and sent vibrations of alarm throughout her body.

"I suggest you take your witless companions and go home, my lady. And if you return, I'll feed you to Berengar's shade."

Behind her Honor heard Wilfred squawk. Theodoric bolted, and the others ran out of the keep after him. De Marlowe was still holding Honor by her sleeve. She'd been trembling while he spoke, but when he mentioned Berengar's shade, her suspicions ignited. She eyed him, ignoring the hollows in his cheeks and the dark smudges under his eyes. Instead she studied the long legs and lean body. Something stirred inside her, a pleasurable feeling that struggled against her alarm. She ignored that as well, and concentrated on her suspicions.

"You!"

De Marlowe looked at her curiously. "Yes?"

"You black-hearted, false churl. There is no shade of Berengar."

He smiled at her, which inflamed her anger even more. Honor yanked her sleeve out of his grasp.

"You're a foul toad, Galen de Marlowe. Go back to your own cursed land."

"I am on my land."

"Liar. You were always a pestilence." Honor jabbed him in the chest with her forefinger. "Working your evil disguisings on my poor servants. Just the kind of foul prank I'd expect of you."

De Marlowe smirked, wiped a finger across her cheek and showed her the white paste that covered it. "I would not speak of disguisings, my lady." He suddenly tugged her wig off and examined it. "What a monstrous ugly thing this is."

He gave her a mocking look, but the smile on his lips faded. Honor eyed him with distrust, but he seemed distracted by her hair. To her amazement he dropped the wig and stretched out his fingers. He gently stroked a length of her copper strands.

"Heed me, my lady ghost. If I find you on my land again, I'll throw you over my saddle and parade you all the way back to your father. I doubt not that the whole countryside will find great amusement at the sight of your little bottom wiggling in the air."

Honor inhaled sharply and glared at him. "Why you—you—Leekshanks!"

"What?"

"You heard me. Leekshanks. By my faith, you're nothing but a common ruffian, and I'll not suffer you on my land another fortnight. May the Holy Trinity deliver me from ever having to come into your foul presence again!"

Honor stormed around her adversary, but as she moved, her foot caught on one of the ragged shreds of her gown as they flapped around her legs. She tripped and would have hit the floor if de Marlowe hadn't caught her. When his arms encircled her, she grabbed them and twisted. They ended up facing each other and both went still. Honor stared up into eyes that no longer seemed hard and angry. A glint came into them, and it stirred an agitation in her that was pleasurable and disquieting.

"By my troth," he whispered. "If all shades had amber hair and felt so soft, I'd welcome them."

Honor swallowed. "You would?"

He bent down and breathed close to her ear. "Yes."

She turned to look at him, and his lips touched hers. Honor froze in surprise as his tongue slipped into her mouth. He pulled away, suddenly stepping back a few paces.

"Ugh. You've got that cursed paste on your lips. What a foul taste."

Honor felt herself redden beneath the paste she

wore. "It serves you right for touching me. I'll not suffer it again, my lord."

"Oh no?"

He came at her, but Honor grabbed her skirts and ran. She reached the door, but he caught her wrist. She clamped her other hand on the door frame and pulled. Her wrist came free suddenly, and she scrambled out of his reach and put her back to the wall beside the door, ready to slip away at the first opportunity. De Marlowe came toward her with an evil smile.

"That will teach you not to make threats you can't support, my lady shade."

He reached for her, but Honor dodged aside and catapulted herself out of the keep. She skittered down the stairs and across the ward. Only when she reached the gatehouse did she dare look back. Galen de Marlowe was leaning in the doorway of the keep, watching her, a lighter shadow against the darkness beyond. His voice floated toward her in the night.

"So, that's the way to rid myself of you. If you wish to avoid my touch, little shade, don't come back to Durance Guarde."

Her heart began to rattle against her rib cage. Honor stared at the tall, dark figure in the doorway for a moment, then turned and ran. She kept running until she was across the dry moat and out of Durance Guarde altogether. She found Wilfred, Jacoba, and Theodoric cowering behind a tree.

"We were so frightened, lady."

"I near pissed in me gown," Theodoric said.

Wilfred was still babbling prayers.

"Quiet, all of you," Honor snapped. "It was all a ruse. De Marlowe admitted it to me, so calm yourselves."

"Oh, lady, oh, lady, oh, lady."

Honor clamped her hand over Jacoba's mouth and stared into the maid's frightened eyes. "I give you my word. It was but a disguise, like our own, done to frighten us. Understand?" Jacoba nodded, and Honor removed her hand.

She turned and began to make her way through the forest, taking care not to stumble over logs or catch her foot on a vine or shrub. The others hurried after her.

"Is he coming after us, lady?" Jacoba asked.

"No. Why would he? He thinks he's frightened us out of Durance Guarde forever."

"But you said he revealed his plot. He must know you won't be frightened again," Theodoric said. "Did he threaten you, me lady?"

"Yes."

Wilfred caught up with her. "Ooo. What did he say?"

"Never you mind. He thinks he's won, but he hasn't."

"Oh, lady, no," Jacoba said. "We can't go back there."

Honor swerved to avoid a bush as tall as she was. "I can go back, and I will. Just not right away.

Not until I have some potent remedy against this knave."

Jacoba groaned. "But, lady—"

"I wish I were a man. I could destroy him." Honor kicked a pile of leaves and stomped over them.

"But, lady—"

Honor stopped and turned on Jacoba. "No protestations, woman. Galen de Marlowe made me play the fool this night, and I mean to pay him for it. I take an oath before God, I'll lead him like a bull with a ring in its nose, for all to see. I swear I will."

With a last glower in the direction of Durance Guarde, Honor plunged onward through the forest. Her companions heard her speak only once during the rest of the journey.

"Leekshanks!"

SIX

❧

ENTIRELY PLEASED WITH himself,
Galen walked his horse through the forest on his
way back from a morning spent fishing for trout. A
stream wound around Durance Guarde and into
the valley that divided his land from the Stafford
demesne. It was deep, clear, and no one lived near
it because in a heavy rain it swelled and flooded
the valley, which suited Galen. He'd caught seven
trout, more than enough for a midday meal.

Since he'd frightened off that nuisance, Honor
Jennings, almost a fortnight ago, he hadn't been
bothered. Except for the dreams of her. They
wouldn't stop, especially now that he'd touched
her. Of all the women he'd been with, none had
remained in his memory simply because of how
their skin felt beneath his fingertips. Honor's skin

was softer than the silk that came on merchant ships across the dangerous seas from India.

Galen looked down at his hand. He was stroking his horse's neck as if it were Honor's, noticed what he was doing and lifted his hand.

"Fool."

He straightened and guided his mount toward the old castle, then pulled up and dismounted in a hollow where a streamlet danced down a ridge covered with trees and underbrush. Near a birch tree he found what he was looking for, lungwort, an herb used to treat maladies of the chest. Ralph had caught a slight cold after he'd posed as Berengar's ghost, and he swore he was about to die. Galen only detected a sniffle, but his manservant had his heart set on suffering. He'd asked for feverfew to treat his headache, lemon balm for the fever he didn't have, and wormwood to aid his digestion and to repel the armies of fleas in his chamber—fleas that Galen never saw.

As he knelt on the ground gathering the herbs, he sighed and wondered how long it would take to forget the softness of Honor's skin. He couldn't remember how Constance's skin had felt anymore. His marriage seemed to have taken place in another lifetime. Honor Jennings had invaded his land and his thoughts, and although he'd banished her from his presence, she haunted him more surely than any unhappy ghost haunted Durance Guarde.

He grinned as he thought of Honor's white

face when she opened the keep door to find him blocking her escape. She had made a little squeaking sound, and her mouth had formed a dark O in the midst of that ridiculous paste she'd slathered over her neck and face. But she hadn't remained frightened for long. She'd always been clever, even as a small girl who followed him around at tournaments, banquets, and weddings.

He never understood why she'd chosen to bedevil him rather than his younger brothers. The twins were nearer her age. He remembered being a youth, burning with eagerness to prove himself a right honorable knight and skilled warrior. Having a small copper-haired child for a shadow when one strode about the pavilions and tents of a royal tournament had been embarrassing.

Galen laughed softly as he stuffed herbs into a pouch and rose from the ground. Once he'd entered his tent during a tournament and found a strange sight—a tiny figure in a bright yellow gown topped by his jousting helmet, stumbling around, arms extended and thrashing blindly. Chuckling at the memory, Galen mounted and rode through the trees toward Durance Guarde.

He was almost there when he heard noise— shouting, clattering, and banging, and above it all, Ralph yelling. He rode through the barbican and across the drawbridge he'd reinforced. Inside he found a dozen men crawling on the walls, clambering up the towers, and hammering at the mortar in the walls. Ralph perched on the keep stair landing and yelled at them without effect.

Honor Jennings stood near the chestnut tree where the blacksmith's shop used to be and listened to a man who held a large piece of parchment. From the square, hammer, and drafting chisel in his belt Galen deduced he was a master mason. The woman was mad! She was planning to build her cursed manor house around him. Galen dismounted and strode over to Honor.

"What do you think you're doing?"

Honor barely glanced at him. "I see what you mean, Master Alfric. We'll simply knock down the keep and build the house there. Can we save the stables? Master Alfric, are you listening?"

Alfric's gaze had fixed on Galen the moment he joined them, and it hadn't wavered. Galen almost growled at her.

"Get out."

Honor ignored him. "Come, Master Alfric. I want to look at the stables." She started walking, but Alfric remained frozen where he was, so she came back and spoke to Galen. "Go about your business, my lord. I have plans to make and no time for interferences from you.

"My lady." Alfric folded the parchment he'd been holding. "You never said someone lived in this place when we spoke in London."

"It matters not," Honor said. "And I marvel at

the great speed of your journey. I thought you'd be at least another month on your previous job."

"By God's mercy!" Galen bellowed.

All the hammering and shouting stopped. The men crawling on the wall walk and hanging out tower windows stopped too.

Honor rounded on him and was about to speak, but Galen shouldered her aside and stalked away.

"Master Alfric, a word with you." When Alfric didn't move, he snapped, "At once."

He stopped by the well and fixed his gaze on the master mason. The man had skin like sun-dried leather and hands scarred from years of working with stone and brick. He waited until the man began to fidget under his gaze, then spoke softly.

"I am Galen de Marlowe. This is my land. Leave."

Alfric twisted his parchment and bowed low. "Oh, Lord de Marlowe, I didn't know. I swear I didn't know this was your land. The lady said—"

"I know what the lady said." Galen folded his arms and glared down at the mason. "Begone and trouble me no more."

"Aye, my lord. At—at once, my lord."

Only too happy to leave, Alfric scurried over to the wall walk, avoided Honor's outraged gaze, and began herding his men out of the castle. Honor watched with narrowed eyes, then marched over to the master mason. Galen had the great pleasure of seeing her wave her arms, point this way and that to no avail.

"This is my land, I tell you."

Shaking his head, Master Alfric shoved his cap down around his ears and hurried after his retreating men. Galen watched his adversary run after the mason, only to trip on the root of the chestnut tree and fall on her face. He burst out with a sharp laugh. He stopped laughing when she failed to jump to her feet as she had all the other times he'd seen her trip. Running over to her, he knelt beside her, his brow furrowed. When he tried to take her in his arms, Honor twisted over onto her back and scowled up at him.

"You horrible man, don't touch me."

"I thought you'd hurt yourself."

Honor shoved his hands away and sat up. "I got the wind knocked out of me, that's all. I'll not have you touch me."

"Why not?" He smiled at the way she tried to brush herself off but merely spread the dust around.

She paused to stare at him. "After what you did to me the last time we met? I've heard about you. I've heard how you enchant women and make them do your bidding. You look at them with those sorcerer's eyes and—and . . ."

"And what?" He smiled again when she reddened.

"Never mind. You put me in great unquietness with your forward ways, my lord. Leave me be."

"You have a smudge on your nose."

She rubbed her nose, then her cheek, transferring the smudge from one place to the other.

Grinning, he picked up the hem of her gown. Honor slapped his hands.

"Stop that and hold still," he commanded.

She watched him warily as he wiped her face. He brushed wisps of her hair back, and his skin slid gently against hers. He couldn't stop himself from brushing her cheek with his fingertips. She was still scowling at him, but his ire had been swallowed up in humor and desire.

"Did you know your skin is as soft as it was when you were a child?"

He heard the rough quality of his voice. Ah, well. It wasn't a surprise. Galen drew closer to her and she retreated, placing her hand flat on his chest.

"What has my skin to do with anything?"

"It has to do with this."

He encircled her with one arm and kissed her. He thought she would pull away, but after a moment's frozen stillness, she opened her mouth. She tasted like cinnamon. He leaned closer and soon they were lying on the ground beneath the chestnut tree. Her arms wrapped around him, and he kissed his way from her lips to her cheek and down her neck. In the space between one breath and another he forgot any outrage that lingered within him. His fingers laced through curls softer than the velvet on a queen's robe. He felt Honor begin to tremble as he kissed the hollow of her throat. She made a tiny noise that sounded as much like surprise as pleasure. Whatever it was it spurred his craving. His mind afire along with his body, he paid no attention when someone cried out.

"My lady!"

Something bashed Galen's ear. "Ow!"

He looked up to find a waiting woman standing over him.

"You get off her at once, or I'll box your ear again, sorcerer or no."

He looked down at Honor. She was hiding her face in the crook of his arm. The waiting woman drew back her fist, but Galen gave her a stern look and pulled back from Honor, noticing that her face had grown crimson. Feeling guilty for taking advantage of a widow, even if she was annoying, he gently released her and stood. He offered his hand, but that harpy of a waiting woman bustled between them and took charge of her mistress.

"Be you well, me lady? Thanks be to God I returned before he—well, thank God is all I will say."

Galen watched the two as they walked across the ward. Honor had yet to speak, in spite of her maid's solicitous questions. Pent-up sensations whipped through his body, and Galen set his jaw in an effort to gain mastery of them.

"Turn back," he whispered, knowing she couldn't hear him. "Turn and look at me."

The two women kept walking. They neared the gatehouse, moved toward the shadows between the towers.

Galen held himself still and murmured, "Look at me."

As she stepped into the shadows, he almost turned away, but at the last moment, Honor Jennings hesitated. He glimpsed the curve of her cheek as she turned, and their eyes met. Something hot and vital jumped across the space between them.

Under his breath Galen murmured, "Honor."

Then she turned and disappeared into the darkness of the gatehouse. As if released from a spell Galen sagged, then dropped to his knees on the spot where they'd lain.

"Dear God." He stared at the earth, at the root that had tripped Honor. "You lackwit. You tried to take her in the dirt in the middle of the ward."

"Lordship?"

Ralph was hovering over him. "Lordship, she just appeared with those dolts and began measuring the place for her manor house. I couldn't stop them."

"Not now, Ralph."

"I told her you'd be back, but she heeded me not."

Galen jumped to his feet. "Quiet, I charge you. Or I'll toss you in the moat." He stomped off to find his horse. Ralph's plaintiff cry resounded after him.

"But the moat's dry, lordship."

SEVEN

IN THE SOLAR at Castle Stafford Honor stared out an open window. It was a clear June morning, crisp with the coolness of winter's lingering grip, but Honor wasn't interested in the day's beauty. She glared in the direction of Durance Guarde; things were not going well. Her latest attempt yesterday to force Galen de Marlowe out by building a house around him had been a disaster, and now there was more unhappy news. She glanced at the letter in her hand. It had come by messenger this morning. Her lovely new printer's press sat at the bottom of the English Channel in the ship that had been carrying it. The Italian merchant who owned the ship had insured the cargo, but delivery of a new press would take many months, perhaps a year.

"Mayhap old Leekshanks cursed the vessel," Honor said aloud.

Dagobert entered carrying a basket of mending, his eyes twinkling with excitement. "Who, my lady?"

"Never mind," Honor said. "Jacoba said Father had a visitor. Who is it?"

Dagobert set the basket down. "Oh, my lady, such a great lord. Came on a giant black destrier, he did. As I passed through the hall I saw him, all dressed in silk and gold jewels and furs and—"

"But who is it?"

"Don't know, me lady."

Dagobert pursed his lips, but Honor knew that bright-eyed look.

"You've been listening to privy conversations again, haven't you? You spied on them, and you do know who it is."

"It's him!"

Honor frowned. "Who? God bless me, you mean de Marlowe?"

"Aye, me lady. I never seen Lord de Marlowe, but you've been talking about him ever so much, and I'm sure it's him."

Jumping up, Honor hurried from the solar with Dagobert at her heels.

"Where are they?"

"By the fire in the hall, me lady."

"I can hardly believe it, by my troth." Honor almost ran downstairs in her haste. "He's come to complain of me to Father."

"Is he truly a sorcerer?" Dagobert asked.

"Don't be foolish," Honor said as she left the stairs.

She stopped abruptly. Dagobert ran into her and almost knocked her over, but she recovered quickly.

"Be careful," she whispered. "I'll not play the clumsy lackwit in front of him again."

"Sorry, me lady."

Honor glared across the hall at the two men by the fire, but her grimace disappeared as she beheld a stranger in an amber silk tunic shot with gold, black hose, and soft leather top boots. A heavy, ornate gold chain was draped across his shoulders, and another encircled his waist. Shafts of light coming through the windows highlighted the sun-bleached strands of his hair. Honor was suddenly transported back to the ward at Durance Guarde. She felt his body bearing her down, pressing hard against her. Immersed in the memory of his lips, she started when Sir Walter turned and saw her.

"Ah, my dear. I was about to send for you. Come, come. You remember Lord Galen de Marlowe of Argent."

Hoping she wasn't flushed, Honor approached them, slowed by the power of that memory. She knew he'd touched her like that only to frighten her into giving up Durance Guarde. She knew his reputation for seducing but never remaining with women. She knew there was little about her to tempt such a man to court her with sincerity. She knew all these things. She'd discussed them with herself late into the night. None of it made a difference. When he had touched her, all her senses fled, and she had been left quivering like a freshly boiled pudding.

Only once before had this happened to her—when Aymer first played the role of suitor. He'd done so throughout their betrothal. Then had come the wedding night, one best forgotten. And afterward, no pretty words, no hours spent together in conversation or other pursuits.

Honor had grown used to loneliness. Now she didn't mind having no one to share her life's path, a partner upon whom to depend, one to whom she could give this great treasure of love hiding inside her. She had put away any useless longings. It had taken her years, but she had done it. And no seducing knave was going to make a fool of her simply because, in a small corner of her soul, she harbored nonsensical desires.

With each step she took toward the fireplace Honor grew more and more angry with herself. By the time she reached her father, she also was furious with Galen de Marlowe for stirring up desires she hadn't felt before and had trouble controlling.

"Honor," Sir Walter said, taking her hand. "Lord de Marlowe heard you'd come home, and he has called to offer a most valuable service."

Eyeing Galen, Honor said, "Indeed?"

De Marlowe leaned against the chimneypiece and gave her a smile of such charm that she blinked. It was a devastating smile, the kind of smile that surely got him accused of working magic on the ladies of the court. That smile shot at her like an arrow, hurtled past her defenses and zinged into her body, setting off clattering chimes of pure desire. Honor dragged her gaze from his lips and forced herself to listen to her father.

"What?" she said faintly.

"Lord Robert de Mora, Earl of Malvern. His lands are in the north, bordering those of the Percys. He has recently succeeded to the title and must marry. Isn't it kind of Lord Galen to take an interest in your welfare?"

Honor narrowed her eyes and hissed, "God save me, you're speaking of a suitor?"

"Not yet, not yet, my dear. Don't be hasty. Lord Galen will speak to him on your behalf at the royal banquet the king is giving after the wedding of his ward, the Countess of Elstow. I vow it's a most happy coincidence that we're all going to attend."

"I'm not going, and I need no help finding a suitor."

"Nonsense," Sir Walter said with a pat on her hand. "Don't be ungracious. You told me Sir Lionel and Lord Andrew were terrible. Said you feared one of them would try to abduct you, and you hated the man the Jennings wanted to match you with. What was his name? Scattergood."

Seething, Honor darted a hot scowl at Galen and found him still smiling at her, but the smile had now turned stiff. It was like the chain he wore, something he put on for show.

"I had not heard of these unsuitable suitors," he said. "You were wise to rid yourself of them. Sir Lionel Titchwell is an evil-minded bastard—your pardon, Lady Honor—and Lord Andrew Swan would begrudge you even a scrap of bread to break your fast."

"Better a miser than a rapacious seducer," Honor snapped.

"Now, my dear," said Sir Walter, "the Earl of Malvern has no reputation as a seducer of women."

Galen arched an eyebrow and gave her an ingenuous look. "Upon my word, Lady Honor, he does not. Rob de Mora is a most courteous and honorable man. As chivalrous as King Arthur."

"Nevertheless, my lord, I decline to accept your offer. I have many arrangements to make before I think of marriage again."

"I'm sure your father will agree that an alliance with the Earl of Malvern is an opportunity not to be missed," Galen said smoothly. "He's a wealthy man in great favor at court, even if he does have Lancastrian connections. He manages to placate both York and Lancaster, a marvelous feat of diplomacy in these troubled times. Such a man would serve as a formidable protector for you and your demesne."

"But I—"

Sir Walter shook a finger at her. "Oh, no, my dear. None of your protests. We're going to

London to meet Lord Robert, and that's my final word. We'll leave in three days' time." Sir Walter stopped and craned his neck to look out the window. "Perkin? Perkin, I see you in that cart. Are those quince saplings? They are, by my troth. Don't you try sneaking away. You wait right there. Pray excuse me, Lord Galen. I won't be a moment."

Sir Walter hurried out of the hall, leaving Honor to glower in impotent fury at her oppressor. She glanced around the hall and found it deserted. Her voice strong and loud, she uttered a curse.

"The devil take you, Galen de Marlowe. What a loathsome thing to do just so you can keep my land."

"What is this about your being a vowess?" Galen asked. "You don't wear the widow's barb, although I vow it's sometimes difficult to discern what you're wearing since most of it looks like old rags."

"My clothing is none of your concern," Honor snapped. "We were speaking of your evil character. It's cowardly of you to try to keep Durance Guarde this way."

With one step Galen was suddenly so close that she could see the gold flecks in those dark-brown eyes. Honor tried to put distance between them, but he caught her arm, held her close, and spoke in a fierce whisper.

"I'm not trying to keep the damned land, Honor. I'm trying to get rid of you."

Twisting her arm to make him release her, she said, "It's the same thing."

"It's not, God help me." He ignored her attempts to make him let her go.

"Pray, why not?"

Without warning she was lifted so that her face was close to his.

"Why not? After yesterday, you surely realize why we must not continue to dispute. Another quarrel like that, and we'll end up in some haystack or barn, naked and—"

"We will not!"

Honor rammed her fists against his chest, and he let her go. She scuttled out of his reach, gasping for breath, but he closed the distance between them. Honor backed up and hit the chimneypiece. Before she could scoot sideways he was on her.

"You may deny what happened, if you like," he said softly. "I'll prove the truth to you."

Honor turned her head aside as he tried to kiss her. He chuckled and kissed her ear. She caught her breath as his tongue touched her earlobe. He breathed into her ear, and Honor's body ignited. She put her arms around his neck and dragged him down. His mouth covered hers, but as suddenly as he'd begun the embrace Galen lifted his head, stepped out of her arms, and strolled over to one of the chairs. In a heated daze, Honor watched him, her mouth working.

Galen leaned against the chair, gripping its back so hard his knuckles whitened. "Now do you see?" She said nothing, and he gave her that sorcerer's smile and looked past her. "Sir Walter. I trust all is well?"

"Yes, dear boy. A small disagreement with the gardener. You know how it is. When a family has worked at one's estate for generations, it's difficult to convince them they don't own it."

Honor listened in a haze of confusion. She hadn't even thought about who might see her with Galen. He'd kissed her, and she'd lost her wits. If he hadn't stepped away when he did, her father would have seen them, and disaster would have ensued. But he'd been aware of everything—the deserted hall, how long her father had been gone.

"So mayhap we could travel to London together," Sir Walter said.

"What?" Honor cried. "No. I'm not going. I—I don't feel well."

"You look well," Sir Walter said. "Why, your color is high. Lovely red cheeks, my dear."

Galen grinned at her. "Indeed, most comely."

She heartily desired to smack that smile off his face, but contented herself with glaring at him.

"If Lady Honor objects to Rob de Mora, I can recommend you to several other honorable and suitable men, Sir Walter. This banquet is a timely opportunity for such delicate introductions."

"I agree."

Feeling as if everyone was contented but her, Honor pounded her fist against the chimneypiece. "By my faith, I do not agree."

"I'm sorry, my dear, but I've decided. We're going to London."

"But—"

"God give me patience!"

Honor jumped at her father's shout. He calmed and bowed to Galen.

"Your pardon, my boy. She tries me most disgracefully."

"You have my sympathy, Sir Walter."

"We'll see you at the banquet, then."

"Until then, may God protect you and your lovely daughter."

Honor could do nothing but fume and silently curse as she watched Galen de Marlowe walk out of the hall. She was going to tackle her father again, but he bustled away and was through the screen in search of Perkin before she could speak. She was left alone, angry, confused, and suffering from a painful feeling of incompleteness, of pleasure cut short. Every time she touched Galen, she wanted more touching, and when she didn't get it, her body ached most dreadfully. The pain of not touching was growing worse.

And the man who provoked the pleasure and the pain had just let her know he didn't want to be the one to do that anymore.

EIGHT

HE HAD LIED to Honor and her father. Galen had never meant to attend the banquet and other festivities surrounding the marriage of the king's ward. Such an appearance would bring him into the king's presence before he could decide what to do about the Tower vision. He had intended to slip into Westminster, talk to Rob de Mora, and introduce him to Sir Walter. Then he would return to Durance Guarde.

The idea had been that, once in London, Honor would be deluged with suitors. A young woman with a fortune, perfect skin, and hair like molten red-gold would never lack suitors. If she didn't like Rob, surely one of the others would please her, and thus she'd have no time to pester him, to be where he was, to infect him like some erotic plague. Just

as important, he could go back to Durance Guarde
without having to see the king.

It was painful to him to be with Edward, knowing what he now knew. Edward was a good king,
and Galen wanted to protect him and his sons. The
king had two young sons, Edward and Richard,
who were barely out of the nursery. It was the possibility that he might be seeing their fate that tortured him so. Yet in the vision the boys were much
older than Edward's sons were now. He could be
wrong about the identity of the boys in the Tower.
Or, as time passed, the vision might change. That
sometimes happened, but not often. As long as he
was uncertain, he couldn't take action. So Galen
had intended his visit to be short.

He hadn't counted on being waylaid by
Edward's heralds when he came out of his town
house two days after he arrived. They'd spirited
him into the palace. Two guards had escorted him
to the royal apartments, and stuck him in a small
room that overlooked the king's private garden.
They'd left him alone, but the men were outside
the door. Edward had no intention of allowing
him to slip away as he had done before.

Galen paced back and forth, but the floorboards
creaked irritatingly, so he leaned on the windowsill and looked down at the garden. White
roses bobbed in the wind. They grew in profusion
along with scarlet lilies, carnations, cowslip and
crown imperials. The place had been deserted, but
the garden gates swung open, and a man strode

into view. Tall and golden-haired, with hooded eyes and an alert expression, Edward Plantagenet moved at the head of a cluster of noblemen in robes brighter than the flowers. Galen recognized the king's brothers, Richard of Gloucester and George, Duke of Clarence. Clarence directed a raptor's gaze at Earl Rivers, the queen's brother. Richard was talking gravely with one of the powerful Percys of Northumberland.

Galen shook his head. Edward had married a commoner, Elizabeth Woodville, and elevated her numerous brothers and sisters to offset the power of great barons like the Earl of Warwick and the Percys. But he'd gone too far, and now most of the powerful men in the country hated the Earl Rivers and anyone by the name of Woodville.

As he watched the interplay of look and gesture, elegant bows and secret glances filled with vitriolic envy, Galen felt the sunlit scene recede. Shadows closed in, and he glimpsed the river Thames, hurtled into the Tower, into blackness, into a small chamber filled with the sweet breath of two innocent, doomed boys. As suddenly as the vision came, it vanished, leaving Galen disoriented and gasping. He opened his eyes and found himself clutching the windowsill. He blinked rapidly at the sunlight.

God's mercy, he thought blindly.

He straightened and pressed his forehead against the glass panes. Desperate to rid himself of the vision, he summoned images of a copper-haired little nuisance, her disheveled gowns concealing a body designed to provoke a far different kind of madness. He'd seen her yesterday from a distance at an archery contest, one of the festivities that surrounded the banquet. Evidently Sir Walter had persuaded her to abandon her widow's weeds in favor of green silk and cloth of silver. She'd been wearing one of those conical headdresses so popular among the ladies of the court. Unfortunately she'd walked beneath the branch of a tree and whacked the steeple-shaped contraption right off her head. He had wanted to go to her when everyone started laughing, but she had vanished into a tent reserved for ladies. When he saw her next, the headress was gone, which was best. She'd plaited her hair and fastened it at the nape of her neck. Galen would have told her to wear it loose, but widows didn't do that, he supposed. He drew in a deep breath and held the image of Honor Jennings in his mind. As long as it was there, the vision remained a hazy cloud of menace in the background of his thoughts.

In the garden Edward was still holding council with his great barons. One of the guards that had escorted Galen appeared near the gate. Edward glanced at him and nodded. Galen cursed as the king dismissed the noblemen who attended him and left the garden.

Still disoriented, Galen gripped the windowsill again and hissed, "By the saints, compose yourself." He groped blindly, and his fingers touched the hard stone of the wall beside the window. The polished surface was almost as smooth as Honor's skin. He tried to recall her voice and grinned when the first memory that came to him was "Leekshanks!"

He inhaled slowly and opened his eyes. Pushing away from the window, he stepped to the middle of the chamber as the door swung open to reveal the king. Galen knelt and bowed his head. Edward stalked into the room, resplendent in a blue velvet robe trimmed with miniver. He stopped in front of Galen, his booted feet planted wide apart.

"So," he growled, "I have to hunt you down like some forest outlaw. By God's teeth, de Marlowe, if you hadn't saved my hide at the Battle of Tewkesbury, I'd have clapped you in the Tower for running off like that."

"Forgive me, your highness."

"Why should I?" Edward asked. "Get up, man. If fawning pleased me, I'd have killed you long ago, by my troth. Besides, I'm going to forgive you."

Galen burrowed his brow. "Sire?"

Swinging around, Edward planted his fists on his hips and barked a laugh at him. "I'm going to forgive you because I've discovered the real reason for your disappearance. By my faith, I never thought to see Galen de Marlowe brought low by a woman, and by such an odd little mite too. Lady Honor Jennings. I tell you, when I heard you'd spoken to her father, I nearly died of apoplexy. You, who swore never to marry again, allying yourself with that book-ridden, scatter-witted little magpie. Ha!"

Galen almost went slack-jawed. "No, no, no, your highness. This is a false rumor." He scowled. "Who has been spying on me, Sire?"

"King's don't reveal their privy agents, de Marlowe. Was it not you who told me once that winning on the battlefield was only half the art of kingship, and that the other half consisted of knowing things before anyone else did?"

"Important things, your highness. Not false gossip and evil report."

"By God's teeth, you're blushing." Edward let out a loud guffaw.

"I didn't leave court to meet Lady Honor, I left because I had—" Galen clamped his mouth shut, steadied himself and went on. "I left because I'd grown weary of intrigue and base maneuvering."

"Then why were you seen courting Sir Walter Stafford's favor?" Edward clapped him on the back. "Admit it. I see how you've languished away from court, my friend. You've lost weight, and you've grown shadows under those eyes the ladies are always simpering about. You've no other worries in this time of peace, so you might as well confess. Lady Honor is the reason for your decline. You're lovesick."

"I'm not lovesick," Galen growled, adding, "Sire."

"I don't believe you."

Curse it, what a miserable snarl his life had become. "I do not love that pestilence of a woman. She's a nuisance. She wants Durance Guarde and is trying to drive me off my own land. She even tried frightening me by posing as the ghost of Rowena. Upon my word, Sire, the woman is a shrew and mad as well."

The king's grin had grown wider.

"I swear it!" Galen cried. "She keeps bursting into Durance Guarde with her servants and masons and laborers. She said she would pull the keep down around my ears. She invades my peace with her tattered gowns and sunset hair, shrieking at me, tripping over tree roots, and . . ."

Galen's voice trailed off as the king's laughter filled the room.

"So you say, de Marlowe."

"She's a vexatious little shrew!"

Edward drew near and said, "What protests, my friend. Every complaint and insult you utter against this woman confirms what I said. I'm right heartily pleased to hear them. And do you know why?"

"No, Sire. The reason escapes me."

"Because you've been a grievous impediment to several matches I wish to make among my nobles, old friend. Until you went away, I couldn't convince the Countess of Elstow to accept the man I'd chosen for her. She pined for you and insisted I bring her to your notice, as her attempts had failed. And she isn't the only one. The Despenser heiress, the widow of the Marquis of Blackstone and one of my own cousins, all of them have hinted to me about you. God's mercy, I'm right glad you're lovesick."

Galen remained silent for a moment, then

repeated slowly, "Sire, I am not lovesick. I—I came here to beg you to intercede on my behalf and match her with someone quickly so that she can no longer berate and assault me."

"You need my help against a woman? I don't believe it."

"I wish to avoid any unpleasant incidents, your highness. Sir Walter is a good man. It's not his fault Lady Honor is so headstrong. Well, mayhap it is, but I don't wish for this quarrel to grow into something more dangerous."

Edward folded his arms and studied Galen. "I see."

"I'm glad, Sire."

"I shall think upon it."

"I'm most grateful, Sire."

"Of course, if you married her, there would be no quarrel."

"No! I mean, that's not the solution, Your Highness."

"It is if I say it is."

His alarm growing, Galen dropped to one knee. "I beg Your Highness to refrain from considering any matches for me. I—I can't marry again." He felt the king's hand on his shoulder.

"I see the pain in your eyes," Edward said quietly. "You still blame yourself for something you could not have foreseen."

Galen winced, but said nothing. The king offered his hand. Galen took it and rose, avoiding Edward's eyes.

Edward went to a table on which rested an enameled jewel casket. He removed a heavy gold chain from it. The links took the form of alternating suns and white enamel roses of York. From it hung a pendant of the white lion, Edward's personal emblem. The king draped the chain over Galen's shoulders.

"You went away before I could give this to you."

Galen touched the white lion. "I've done nothing to deserve the collar of honor, Sire."

"Did you not warn me that Louis of France was arming the Lancastrians again? I'll hear no protests. You won't let me give you an earldom, so you must take my gifts instead."

"With earldoms come rivals, jealousy, and the possibility of having to fight to keep one's position. I'm sick of war, Your Highness."

"As am I, my friend." Edward sat in the room's single chair, which was draped with purple velvet embroidered with the royal arms. "Now, about Lady Honor. Isidore Jennings has complained to me that she's become a vowess rather than marry the man of his choice or suitors such as Sir Lionel Titchwell or Lord Andrew Swan. The vows can be set aside, of course, and one of them should do."

"Oh, no, Your Highness. Titchwell's a bloody-minded bastard and Swan still has every ha'penny that ever entered his coffers. Neither of them is worthy of the lady, nor are they fit to govern the Stafford demesne."

"Very well. I know of several knights in need of

land. There's old Harold Tiptoft. And there's the Marquis of Langford, and young Colin Wentworth will soon need a bride.

"Wentworth is but seventeen, Sire!"

"Is he?"

Edward's gaze strayed to a silver flagon beside the jewel casket. He gestured, and Galen poured wine into a mazer drinking bowl. Handing the wine to the king, Galen continued. "And Sir Harold Tiptoft is fifty."

"But spry," the king said. He sipped his wine and grinned at Galen. "We went carousing together not a fortnight ago, and he outlasted all my younger companions."

"I beg your forgiveness, Sire, but that's hardly a recommendation. Lady Honor deserves a man who can . . ." Galen eyed the king. "Your Highness is mocking me."

"Mayhap."

Edward handed Galen the mazer and rose. "But you can't have it both ways, old friend. Either you want the lady for yourself, or you want nothing to do with her. If you wish to have nothing to do with her, you can't very well choose her next husband. That, my dear Galen, is a matter for her father and me."

"But, Sire, I was thinking of Rob de Mora."

"I have plans for Rob. In any case, his family would never agree to so lowly a match. No, Galen. There are many things to consider when making

such an alliance. I'll speak to Sir Walter about it
before he leaves town. We should be able to settle
things quickly." Edward opened the door and
glanced at Galen. "I think Langford will do nicely.
He's a good fighter, not greedy, about your age."

Galen's mouth fell open. The Marquis of
Langford had kept the same mistress for all twelve
years of his first marriage. He had seven illegiti-
mate children by her and would never love anyone else. Before he could protest, the king was
gone. Galen slammed the mazer down on the
table, and wine sloshed out of the cup.

"Damnation and siN!"

Rubbing his brow, he prowled the room. His
plan had come to ruin, and he wasn't quite sure
why. He hadn't thought beyond a way to extricate
himself from this fell attraction he had for Honor
Jennings. He had rushed into this scheme, clutching at it without thinking upon the implications.
The result was that he'd thrust Honor into the
path of the king, and she would become what
she'd sought to avoid—a pawn in the shifting,
treacherous game of political alliances that made
the court such a dangerous place. It was said that
often haste rues, and in this case, he was ruing his
haste right heartily.

"What am I going to do?"

"M'lord?"

Galen turned to find that one of the guards had
entered.

"Nothing," he said.

"His Highness says yer to come to the banquet tomorrow night, m'lord."

"I'm not feeling well."

"The king said we wasn't to pay no heed to yer protests," the man said. He was one of those large, stolid individuals who moved through the world with much deliberation. "If yer ill, I'm to fetch a stretcher and carry you to the feast."

"Are you, by God's mercy?"

"Aye, m'lord," the guard said seriously.

"Then I'll be going."

"And so will we, m'lord." The guard stood aside as Galen left the chamber and found the other sentry waiting. He glanced from one to the other. "You're coming to my town house with me, aren't you?"

"Aye, m'lord, and anywhere else ye might wish to go. I'm Miles and this is Cyril. Yer safe with us."

Galen threw up his hands in exasperation. "I'm not in any danger. I don't need you."

"Shall I fetch yer 'orse, m'lord?" asked Miles.

Noting Miles' imperturbable expression and massive build, Galen sighed and nodded. Miles stood aside and bowed.

"After you, m'lord de Marlowe."

"God deliver me," Galen muttered as he went past the man.

"If he don't, m'lord, I will."

that God-cursed cone Father had insisted she wear. After she'd knocked it off and everyone had laughed at her, he had given up pestering her about the way she dressed. That was why this evening she was wearing no hennin, no forked headdress, no long veils supported by wires, or any other uncomfortable contrivance. She'd combed her hair, allowed it to hang loose and dressed it with a gold chain. Aymer had given it to her. Rather, he'd sent it to her one Christmas when he was at court and she was at home as usual. In the French fashion, a sapphire pendant hung from the chain at the center of her forehead, and that was the extent of the headgear she was willing to endure.

She made sure her skirts hung correctly. It wouldn't do to trip over her hem. Then she headed for the great hall. So far she'd managed to find fault with every man Father had thrown her way, and to her surprise, the king showed no inclination to meddle in her marriage plans, or lack of them. She'd thought about this and decided he was simply too busy at the moment to spare her a thought. Her best course was to keep quiet and run back to Castle Stafford at the first opportunity.

Now, if she could just turn her thoughts from Galen de Marlowe, her troubles would be over. She'd lost count of the times she'd struggled with her feelings for that cursed man. He'd been unbearably high-handed, showing up at her home and trying to arrange a match with her father just to keep her from claiming Durance Guarde. And then to touch her the way he had, right in the hall! She'd made a fool of herself with him, but she wouldn't do it again. She didn't understand him. He tried mightily to get rid of her, then acted as if he couldn't keep from kissing her. She was beginning to suspect that he was toying with her—and worse, that she was allowing herself to be played with.

Honor shook her head as she walked down a long corridor lined with royal guards. She thought about Galen all the time now, and she was afraid of the craving the thoughts wakened within her.

He was trying to confuse her. He had some twisted plan in mind to defeat her, and part of it included enticing her with his lean warrior's body. He'd succeeded, much to her alarm. The sight of him set her on fire. Such a thing had never happened to her before. She'd been so young when she'd married Aymer that her initial feelings for him had been more like vague yearnings. Nothing about the way Galen made her feel was vague. Ungovernable, violent, hot and heady sensations rampaged through her body when she beheld him.

A sudden thought made Honor pause in the dark corridor. What if the tales she'd heard from neighbors and courtiers about him were true and Galen was a sorcerer? There had never been any incident to prove he was. No one had ever openly accused a de Marlowe of sorcery. All that had ever existed were rumors and vague suspicions. And Galen's air of mysterious gravity that drove court ladies to distraction. Honor had always scoffed at women who seemed attracted to men because of their dangerous reputations. But what if there was more to the de Marlowe reputation than mere titillating gossip? Had Galen cast some spell on her? Yes. That must be why he had this power over her. He'd worked some fell magic to enslave her.

"Heaven protect me," she muttered. "But why?"

Why would he want to cast a love spell on her? He wanted to be rid of her. It didn't make sense. Nothing about Galen de Marlowe made sense. Mayhap that was because he was a sorcerer. Sorcerers were enigmatic and complex beings. And if he'd cast a spell, these frightening feelings weren't real.

"By my faith, that evil knave is trying to drive me mad!"

What a hideous plot.

"I'll find him this moment and make him remove the spell."

Honor charged into the great hall and paused as the din of hundreds of voices hit her. At one end, before the screen, the royal table had been placed on a dais. Dozens of trestles covered with fine white cloths sat at right angles to it. Each table bore gold and silver flagons, drinking cups of precious Venetian glass or gilded goblets. Before the dais entertainers performed—jugglers, minstrels, acrobats, conjurers, and dancers plied their crafts in the midst of a parade of enormous trays of food borne by royal servants.

A sewer, who would serve her at the table, appeared before her and conducted Honor to her place at one of the trestles. She sat down next to an old lady who was busy dismembering a roasted quail. The place on her right was empty. Honor searched the tables for Galen de Marlowe.

He wouldn't be on the dais, which was reserved for those of highest rank. The king sat there with the queen and the Dukes of Gloucester and Clarence, the Countess of Henlow and her new husband. Honor was craning her neck to see past lofty hennins that bobbed and weaved as their wearers moved. Without warning Galen sat down beside her and grabbed some manchet bread.

"Good e'en to you, Lady Honor."

Honor gasped. "Don't do that."

"You're not eating." He filled a mazer with wine from a flagon and held it out to her.

She scowled at him. "How can you sit there and behave as if nothing has happened?"

"Nothing has happened." He drank some wine and set the mazer on the table. "Not yet. Now, however, I am eating."

He produced his eating knife, cut a slice of roasted egret and popped it in his mouth. Fuming, Honor watched him. He smiled and leaned close to her.

"I've missed you, my little sunset."

"Don't call me that."

"By my troth, you're testy this evening."

Honor opened her mouth, but a blast of trumpets sounded to announce the next course. Servants paraded into the hall to music. They carried large trays bearing peacocks and swans whose feathers had been replaced after the birds had been cooked. Each bird's beak had been covered with gold foil. The sewer at their table carved a peacock and presented a steaming portion to them. Galen cut a few dainty slices and placed them on her trencher. Honor sniffed and turned up her nose.

"I'm not hungry."

"You are too. Your mouth is practically watering, and . . ." Galen put a hand to his ear. "Yes, yes, I hear your stomach growling."

"It is not," she ground out between stiff jaws. The man was impossible.

Before she could tell him so, Isidore Jennings appeared. "Honor, de Marlowe, good e'en to you both."

While Galen rose to greet her brother-in-law, Honor picked up a morsel of peacock and stuffed it in her mouth so she wouldn't have to talk to either man. Isidore was a thin, dry man with the Jennings' black hair and eyes that never rested on one thing for long. Those ever-shifting eyes made Honor uneasy. She remembered how he'd watched her for months after Aymer died. Watched her stomach, rather. He'd been fearful that she would produce a posthumous heir and he'd lose the Jennings' inheritance. Honor couldn't tell him his vigilance was unwarranted: She would never tell him, or anyone, of the tottering, cooing babes that peopled her dreams.

"I've heard rumors about you, Honor," Isidore said.

"What?" Caught off guard, she realized both men were looking at her. "What rumors?"

"That you're to renounce your vows and marry," Isidore replied. His gaze flitted over her head, over her shoulder, everywhere but to her face. "I hope your vows weren't a ruse to avoid marriage with my cousin. An alliance with Sir Drogo Scattergood would be most advantageous."

Galen picked up his eating knife and skewered a piece of meat. "Advantageous to you, mayhap. However, I doubt Lady Honor wishes to connect herself with a man who owes a prince's fortune to the de Medici bank."

"How did you—that's a lie," Isidore cried, his face turning the color of old beets.

Galen set his knife down, turned to Isidore with a sweet smile and said quietly, "By God's mercy, my lord, are you calling me a liar?"

The beet color in Isidore's face faded until it was nearly as pale as the manchet bread. He shook his head rapidly and took a step backward.

"No, no. But Honor must be guided by me if she renounces her vows."

Galen shook his head, still smiling like a cherub, but his hand strayed to the gold and ruby hilt of his dagger. Honor rose and stepped between the two men.

"I've had enough of you two speaking of me as if I weren't here."

Galen said nothing and continued to stare at Isidore. For once Isidore's eyes stopped wandering and fixed warily on his suddenly menacing adversary.

"Methinks I've been deceived," Isidore muttered, but he looked at Honor when he said it.

"By my troth, you have not," she said. "I intend to remain a vowess."

"Dressed in blue silk with gold stars embroidered on it?" Isidore asked with a quick look at her gown.

Galen's eyes narrowed. "Lady Honor's future is none of your concern, Jennings, and neither is her manner of dress."

"I'll complain to the king," Isidore vowed while his gaze began to dart in all directions again.

Honor's heart tried to crawl up her throat. She swallowed hard and she gave Galen a look of mute appeal.

"Jennings, you vex me grievously," Galen said in a low voice. "Keep your mouth shut regarding Lady Honor, or by my faith I'll issue a challenge to you."

Honor saw images of two knights thundering toward each other, lances couched. If their aim was off by a finger's width, the lance tip could glance off plate armor and splinter. A splintered lance could shoot through the eye holes of a visor and pierce the skull, the throat—Galen's throat.

"No!"

Without thinking she put her hand on Galen's

arm, but he ignored her and held Isidore trapped in a killer's gaze. Isidore's jaw set, and Honor was certain he'd be foolish enough to risk a fight. Then his gaze strayed to the gold collar of honor gracing his opponent's shoulders. Honor noticed it too for the first time. King Edward's collar of honor. She almost smiled when Isidore cleared his throat.

"It's not worth my trouble," he said. "I'll not dispute with you over so paltry a matter, de Marlowe. Good e'en."

Honor sighed and said, "Thanks be to God." She rounded on Galen. "What possessed you? Isidore isn't a great warrior, but he doesn't have to be. He fights most unchivalrously."

"Am I to go in dread and fear intolerable because Jennings fights like a street thief?"

Galen glanced at her hand on his arm and something stirred in his eyes. Honor lifted her hand as if it touched a hot anvil, and Galen whispered to her, "By God's mercy, little sunset. You were afeared for me."

"I was not."

Honor plumped herself back down on her stool and jabbed her spoon into a dish. It was a pottage of herbs—borage, kale, bugloss, parsley, violets and such in broth with hare meat. Galen sat down beside her and dipped his spoon in the dish too.

"You were," he said.

"Was not."

"You grew wan and near toppled over in a faint."

Honor threw her spoon down and hissed, "Saints spare me, I'm sorely vexed with your ridiculous imaginings, my lord."

Then she narrowed her eyes and studied him. He was eating calmly, his elegant hands moving with grace, his manners perfect. He seemed so certain. Was it because he'd caused her to quiver in fear for his life? She sucked in her breath. He was magicking her again! She wouldn't have it. Not a bit longer. She felt his power even now, coursing through her body, making her want him, driving her. Making her crave the touch of his hands. God's mercy, she couldn't keep her eyes from those beautiful hands.

Honor shook herself and glared at him. She could feel her face grow hot, and the heat was spreading down her neck and to privy places in her body. The evil churl.

"My lord!"

Galen winced. "You needn't shout in my ear. I can hear you perfectly well. Have some capon."

Honor glared at the slice of capon he offered on his knife, picked up her spoon and knocked it away. The capon flew across the table and landed on the sleeve of Lady Whiffle. The lady didn't notice because her attention was riveted on the conjurer who was in the midst of making a rabbit vanish from the cap of the Duke of Clarence.

"I want no capon, nor egret, nor any of your attentions. I know what you're about, my lord."

"You do?" He smiled at her and moved his knife

away from her spoon. "Tell me so that we'll both be privy to the secret."

He was baiting her. Honor gritted her teeth and said, "Not here." She glanced at the old lady beside her, whose attention had strayed from a troupe of acrobats to Honor. Honor lowered her voice.

"I would have privy speech with you, my lord. And speedily."

Galen studied her for a while, then turned and took a flagon of wine from the sewer. He poured a dark red liquid into a glass goblet and handed it to her.

Her patience gone, Honor took it and said, "Meet me in the royal gardens by the cherry tree." She flushed as she heard his low laughter.

"You've not had practice at this. Meet me there, and we'll have the company of two dozen other illicit couples."

"Indeed," she snapped. "I have not had practice at meeting plumped-up knaves, but I must need do it this once."

Galen bent his head and whispered, "Then go to the garden and out the small door in the southwest corner, by the old birch tree. There's a flagstone path that leads to the plum orchard and then to the menagerie. Meet me at the center of the orchard, by the wishing well. Where are you going?"

"To the garden."

"Not at once, my little addlepate." He straightened and began to watch the conjurer. Sipping his wine, he continued, "Wait until the trumpets announce the next course. There will be a dozen subtleties, marchpane castles, and sugar dragons and the like. When everyone is marveling at them, slip away. I'll follow you in a while."

"I vow you've done this before, sneaking away to meet a lady," Honor said, none too pleased.

"Chivalry prevents me from discussing it, my little sunset, but your interest in my affairs is most flattering."

"I'm not interested in your conquests of women!"

"Shh."

"And don't hush me as if I were a child." Honor wanted to smack that smile off his face. "Oh, the devil take you."

Turning her face away, she directed her gaze toward the conjurer and tried to eat with ease and grace, the way he did, instead of jabbing at meat and pasties as if they were her enemies. She stewed and fumed for what seemed like hours, every pore and inch of her skin alive and sensitive to his presence. At last the trumpets sounded. She rose, and started when Galen put his arm out to block her.

"Take your arm from me, my lord."

He bent and moved the stool on which she'd been sitting, freeing her gown from its legs. He looked up at her, grinning. "God forbid that I should allow you to pitch over on your face in front of all the court. I prefer you to do it when I can help you as I did at Durance Guarde."

"Oh! May God preserve me."

Honor yanked her skirts from his grasp and scurried away from him. She didn't stop until she reached an archway. There she turned and looked back. Galen had risen and was leaning on the table looking at a beautiful blonde woman who'd just walked up to him. She laughed and offered her hand. Galen bowed and kissed it. Honor hesitated, but Galen never looked in her direction. When the lady came close to touch the gold collar Galen wore, Honor sniffed, whipped around and marched out of the hall.

By the Trinity, he was brazen. He was all courtliness and grace to that insipid white rat of a woman trying to catch his favor. Honor thought about the lady's fashionably pale hair, and jealousy curdled her heart. What new magic torture was this? Galen had no sooner finished ensorcelling her than he worked his wiles on another lady. Lady Honor Jennings wasn't going to fall prey to him like that bold harlot, like all the others she'd heard about. She would remind him he was nothing but silly old Leekshanks, and he could take his spells and his pretty face and go elsewhere. By God's mercy, he could.

Honor picked up her skirts and stalked down a corridor toward a side door. "He thinks he's brought me right low and weak with his trickery. I'll teach him. I'll reduce him to a quavering kitchen scurvy, I will. He'll rue the day he tried to enchant me."

TEN

WHILE HE PRETENDED to listen to the flattery of Lady Nicolette, Galen strove to master himself. He wasn't used to being unable to govern his emotions; at least, outside his visions. Yet tonight he'd nearly challenged that pasty-faced dullard Isidore Jennings. The man would have matched sweet Honor with Drogo Scattergood, the greatest wastrel in the kingdom. And Isidore hated Honor. How could anyone hate Honor, with her lively, clever wit and reckless courage? Anyone could see she'd make an excellent wife to a well-placed nobleman, one who deserved her, of course. The trouble was, there weren't many that did.

Galen endured through the tasting of the subtlety placed before him. He served Lady Nicolette, who wouldn't go away. When she had her mouth full, he murmured an excuse and scooted off his stool. He was gone before she could swallow and protest. Slipping behind an arras, he found himself in a deserted passageway lit by a candle in a wall sconce. He headed for a door, had his hand on the latch, when he heard someone call his name. With a guard in Jennings livery, Isidore scuttled into the passage, his hand on his dagger.

"If I were you, my lord, I'd pay more attention to my own affairs and less to those of the Jennings family."

Galen eyed the man-at-arms, cursing the fact that one didn't attend royal feasts wearing battle swords. The weapon at his side was ceremonial, and wouldn't match the one carried by the guard.

"Are you planning to murder me at King Edward's banquet, Jennings?"

"What provokes you to say such a thing? I merely warn."

Jennings and his man moved toward Galen. The arras moved again, and two more men appeared.

"For the ease of my heart, I must convince you to leave the apportioning of the Stafford inheritance to me," Isidore hissed.

Galen crossed his arms over his chest and looked past Jennings at the two newcomers. "Did you hear? Jennings has an uneasy heart."

The men behind Isidore shrugged. Jennings whipped around and tried to draw his sword. The guard did the same, but their opponents already held theirs.

The taller of the two newcomers cocked his head. "Uneasy in your heart, Jennings? Let me cut it out for you. That should banish the discomfort."

Isidore's gaze darted from one to the other of his adversaries. Then he signaled to his guard, who sheathed his half-drawn sword. He scuttled around the two men, toward the arras. "Remember what I said, de Marlowe. The Stafford inheritance is mine."

Galen uncrossed his arms and headed for Isidore, but Jennings darted through the arras along with the guard, and the two newcomers blocked his way. At the same time, Galen felt the world around him recede. He halted abruptly, staring at a distant scene. He glimpsed a man riding beside a river on a fine black hunter, then the vision faded abruptly. Had the man been Aymer Jennings? Why was he seeing visions of Aymer Jennings, who had been dead for years?

Confused, he shook his head. The scene had appeared and vanished in seconds, leaving him disturbed but unable to discern its significance. Neither of his companions had noticed his distraction. One of the men grabbed Galen and crushed him in a rough hug.

"Jesu, Galen, it's good to see you. What did you do to anger Isidore Jennings?"

Galen gasped and shoved him away. "Let go, Macaire. You're breaking my ribs."

Macaire de Marlowe was in a good humor, as

usual, and as usual his cheerfulness in the midst of Galen's adversity was irritating. Four years younger than Galen, Macaire had an optimistic nature which made his gift for speaking to other people with his mind less of a burden than Galen's much different talent. Galen had decided long ago that Macaire found it easy to bear his gift because he simply refrained from employing it. Ignoring difficulties sometimes made them go away.

Macaire released his brother and grinned. "First you say you're sick to death of intrigue and fighting, and then you stir up trouble with that arse. How are you?"

"Sore in my ribs," Galen said, rubbing his side. "Well met, Fabron."

The slim, dark young man beside Macaire sheathed his sword. "Well met, beloved brother. Are you crazed in your mind or have you become suddenly enamored of adversity and death?"

Fabron, and his twin Fulk, were but six and twenty, but Fabron had a spiteful turn of phrase. Galen scowled, trying to fight off the disorientation of that fleeting vision of Aymer Jennings. He didn't like the fact that the vision of the dead man had appeared after he'd been with Honor. Something might be wrong. Or perhaps his difficulties with Honor had brought up old memories he'd forgotten.

"What are you talking about?" he asked.

Fabron glanced at Macaire, who had grown silent and looked unhappy.

"Abandoning court is foolish enough," Fabron said, "but going to ground at Durance Guarde of all places, and spreading those old tales of ghosts. Deliberately making the place seem haunted. You'll get us all accused of witchcraft."

"I didn't do anything."

"We heard the rumors all the way in Argent," Macaire said.

"That wasn't me," Galen replied. "Lady Honor Jennings was trying to roust me from Durance Guarde and claim it for herself. She disguised herself as the ghost of Rowena."

Fabron tossed his glossy black hair back from his face. "She wouldn't have done it if you'd been at Argent, where you belong. Come home. We're tired of looking after the place for you."

"I'm not coming home for a while. I can't."

His brothers stared at him, and Galen looked away. Fabron often made him uncomfortable, for his gift was to sense emotions. It was damned disconcerting to have a younger brother who knew how you felt, especially if you desired a woman or were frightened about something. There had been times during their youth when Galen had been forced to box Fabron's ears for announcing some embarrassing truth to the whole family.

Macaire said to Fabron, "It's a vision."

"It's more than a vision," said Fabron.

Galen rolled his eyes.

"But it's mostly a vision," Macaire said.

Fabron shrugged. "He must face it."

"You don't have them," Macaire said. "You don't understand."

"I understand he has a duty not to expose the family to talk that could lead to danger."

"He would never do that."

"He's damned near done it already," Fabron snapped. Galen's growl stopped him from saying more.

"God's mercy! I can't help it if Honor Jennings makes more noise and chaos than a Lancastrian army. I'm trying to find a remedy."

"Simon sent us with a message," Fabron said, unfazed by Galen's wrath. "He says King Edward is grievously unhappy at your absence and you must remain at court now that you're back. I disagree. I think you should come home."

"Damn Simon and his opinions." Simon had been born two years after Galen. He had the ability to see patterns of events, and an uncanny talent for sensing danger and evil, which made him think he had the right to tell his brothers what to do. For their own good, of course.

Macaire drummed his fingers on his sword hilt. "I'm glad I don't have visions. You have a troublesome gift, Galen." He glanced at Fabron. "He won't come home."

"He must," Fabron said with a grim expression. "Simon has told us there are signs of distant trouble. We need time to prepare, and by God, Galen, this is no time for weakness."

Galen reached out and lightly slapped Fabron's

clean-shaven cheek. "I remember you in swaddling clothes, and dirty ones at that, my sweet brother. Don't talk to me of weakness."

Fabron gave him a malicious smile. "Then don't involve yourself in this affair between the Staffords and the Jennings. I've always thought there was something odd about Aymer Jennings' death, and now you're battling with his widow."

"I grow weary of everyone accusing me of things I haven't done." Galen sighed. "Listen to me, my dear brothers. I'm not coming home. I will settle this dispute with Lady Honor, and I will remain at Durance Guarde."

"For how long?" Macaire asked.

"I don't know. Now, run along. I'm meeting the lady in the plum orchard, if she hasn't fled by now." When his brothers exchanged knowing glances, he cursed. "It's not like that, damn you. Keep your foul imaginings for harlots and leave Honor Jennings out of them, or by my troth, I'll whip them out of you."

Macaire whistled, and Fabron smirked. Galen stalked toward them, and they backed away quickly.

"Be off with you!"

Macaire laughed and darted through the arras. Fabron held the tapestry in one hand and paused, surveying Galen. Without warning he put his hand over Galen's heart. Into his eyes came a faraway look, as if he were listening to the whispers of invisible companions. His hand contorted, twisting in the fabric of Galen's tunic.

"Marvels and wonders, dear brother." Then Fabron's eyes focused on Galen, and he whispered with certainty, "You're besotted. Lovesick, pale and pining, full of heart's torment, wan and parlous, simple-witted with desire."

Galen knocked Fabron's hand away. "Don't touch me like that, Fabron. We swore never to use our gifts against one another."

Fabron was calm in the face of his older brother's anger.

"I but seek to enlighten. You seem to be thrashing in the dark, floundering in a sea of confusion. Leave the past where it should be—in graves—and open yourself to what is offered."

His body rigid, Galen said, his voice growing louder, "Get out before I kick you out on your arse."

The trouble with having a brother who could literally read one's heart was that he never believed one's idle threats. Fabron blew a kiss just to annoy him and was gone. Breathing hard, Galen muttered another curse and stalked outside. He walked into the royal garden, past an arbor where a couple sat kissing. He hurried down a path between beds of white roses that seemed to glow in the darkness, and went out the narrow door he'd described to Honor. Now he was outside the walled garden with only moonlight to guide him. His booted foot found the flagstone path, and he walked down it, attempting to master the foul mood the confrontation with Jennings and his brothers had engendered.

This was exactly why he'd left court. It was inhabited by powerful magnates, their armed companions and adherents, and countless lesser barons. Their shifting loyalties and backroom intrigues sickened him. Worst of all, the court was a hotbed of rumor and backstabbing. Ruthless nobles took advantage of any weakness or disorganization in the royal government to pursue their own ends, and often engaged in outright thievery. Or worse.

It was clear that Honor had become the object of contention among these ruthless men, some of whom—like Isidore Jennings—were as lawless as any highwayman, only with better clothes. This was why women needed the protection of marriage. He didn't understand why Honor couldn't see that, choose a new husband and go away. He had to convince her of the logic of this reasoning. If she went to her new husband's lands, he wouldn't have to suffer the agony of seeing her without being able to . . . Best not pursue the thought.

Galen entered the plum orchard, row upon row of fruit-laden trees. Clouds drifted across the moon overhead and sailed on, wraithlike, driven by unseen winds. He'd forgotten how deserted the orchard was at night. Toward the center the trees grew closer together, shutting out the moonlight.

Had Honor been frightened of the blackness? Mayhap not, for she'd skulked about Durance Guarde on blacker nights. But she hadn't been alone.

At last the clouds drifted away from the moon and he saw her. She was standing beside the stone wishing well in the clearing at the center of the orchard. He toyed with the idea of circling around and coming into the well clearing across from the flagstone path, but discarded the idea. Honor seemed to be angry with him for some new reason, something important enough to cause her to risk speaking to him alone. Frightening her would be rude and mean, and he found himself less and less inclined to be either where she was concerned.

So he left the shelter of the plum trees and walked across the small, flagstone plaza in the center of which lay the wishing well. Honor had been peering into the depths of the well, but when she heard his footsteps she straightened to face him.

"God's mercy, you were an age. Did that lady with the whitewashed hair detain you?"

"What lady? Oh, Lady Nicolette. No, I was waylaid by my brothers, who wish me to come home. They dislike governing Argent in my absence, the lazy sots."

Galen joined her at the well and immediately became distracted by the way the moon highlighted her skin with a silver luminescence. He caught his breath and remembered his resolve.

Taking her hand, he brushed his lips across it

and murmured, "I am my lady's humble servant. You wished to speak to me. You have but to express your wish. I am at your command."

"Oh!" Honor jerked her hand out of his, scuttled away from him and pounded her fist on the lip of the well. "By my faith, you're trying to drive me mad so that you can be rid of me, and I—"

"No."

She looked at him with an expression of astonishment.

"No?" she squeaked.

"No." Galen ran a hand through his hair. "No. I'm simply trying to find a good man who will protect you. Haven't you seen it tonight? The vultures are circling, Honor. The Stafford lands aren't enormous, but they're passing rich and well situated near Westminster and London. Jennings suspects your vows are a sham. God's mercy, I don't think he would let them stand in his way. He's biding his time, probably hoping to obtain Sir Walter's complicity in his schemes. I've been trying to make you understand this."

"Liar." She was sneering. "You went to my father behind my back with your own scheme."

"Mayhap at first, but I've seen too many men looking at you with speculation, and believe me, my lady, their interest has to do with crop yields and florins, not your charms. Now, the king forbids us to consider Rob de Mora, but I know several fine men. There's the Earl of Raveley, Baron

Wakefield, and Lord Peter Fortescue. Wakefield's a bit old, but he's hale, and the other two are good, strong, and kind." He would have gone on, but Honor stomped her foot and uttered a small roar.

"God give me strength!" She drew herself up to her full height and said, "Stop it. Stop it, stop it. You babble on and on about suitors and marrying me off when all the time you're working your evil upon me."

Galen stared at her, bewildered. "You're not making sense. I'm not working any evil." By the moonlight he could see her eyes become slits.

"You know what you've done," she said in a deadly tone. "Don't pretend you haven't worked some enchantment."

He spread his arms. "*What* enchantment?"

She wasn't listening to him. Honor made a fist and beat it against her stomach in a distracted manner. "I can feel it even now. Strange, maddening sensations. And the heat. It crawls through me whenever you appear. I know it's your doing, because the closer you come, the hotter the flames."

Galen studied her; indignation and confusion made her seem even more appealing than usual. What did she mean by this talk of crawling heat? Then, in an instant, he understood what she was trying to tell him.

"Damnation and sin," he said softly. "You really think I've worked a spell on you." He drew nearer, almost laughing, but afraid he'd hurt her if he did.

"My sweet little sunset, what you're experiencing is desire, unaided by magic of any sort." He placed his lips close to her ear and breathed the words "Plain, ordinary lust."

She gasped and jumped back to glare at him in outrage.

"It is not, and you're an evil-minded, corrupt man to say such a thing."

Galen laughed and shook his head, then slipped his arm around her waist and drew her to him. Caught off guard, she froze and stared up at him. He dragged her against him so that their lips almost touched.

"If you don't believe me, I'll have to prove it to you."

ELEVEN

HONOR SAW GALEN as a dark shadow against the lighter darkness of the sky. His mouth touched hers lightly, and although he held her against his body, all he did was skim his lips lightly over her cheek to her ear. She caught her breath when his tongue touched her earlobe. His breath invaded and set her blood churning.

In moments she forgot her wrath. Primitive urges whipped around her body when she felt his leg nudge between hers. He pressed her against the side of the well, and his hand slid down her side to caress her hip. Then his hips pressed against hers, and she realized with a jolt what would come next. Pleasure vanished.

"No," she said in a hoarse voice, and she twisted out of his grasp.

Galen moaned, gripped the well ledge and bent down as if in pain. Honor touched her flaming cheeks and rounded on him.

"There—" Her voice cracked, and she had to start over. "There, you see. Take your devil's magic away. I demand it."

Galen was still bent, breathing hard and silent. Finally he turned his head and shook it.

"You won't? I'll go to my father. I swear it."

He held up a hand. "A moment more, I beg you." Straightening, he turned away from her and seemed to be engaged in some inner struggle.

"Well?" Honor demanded.

Galen faced her, and Honor was confused to see his brow furrowed.

"Honor, my little sunset, did you not experience these same feelings when your husband—that is, in your marriage bed?" He threw up his hands in exasperation. "Didn't your husband make you feel—" He looked up at the sky. "God's mercy, I can't say it."

Honor was beginning to understand, and she backed away. "I don't wish to hear more, in any case."

Galen grabbed her hand to prevent her from leaving.

"No, wait. You must listen to me."

She tried unsuccessfully to free herself. "I don't want to listen."

"It's for your welfare," he said, and he grabbed her other hand. Drawing her close, he whispered,

"I give you my solemn oath before God. I've used no enchantment on you. I know nothing of such arts. And listen to me, Honor Jennings. What you feel, what I feel, it's quite ordinary, yet a wondrous gift from God. It is the natural attraction between a woman and a man."

Thoroughly humiliated by her ignorance, Honor stared at the ground in silence.

"And if Aymer Jennings failed to give this gift to you, it was because he was a selfish, callous bastard."

"No," Honor said in a little voice. "It was because I'm not pleasing in appearance or manner."

"Ridiculous."

"I have no grace or courtliness, no feminine attractions." She stopped because he placed his fingers against her lips.

Coming close again, he shook his head gently, removed his fingers and replaced them with his lips. This time she submerged into a dark, hot place that threatened to envelop her completely. She felt his fingers touch her neck and brush her face. Galen lifted his lips and placed his hands on either side of her face.

"God help me, I find you the most fascinating and arousing little termagant in the kingdom."

"Termagant?" she murmured, her thoughts fuzzy and unfocused.

Galen smiled and traced the line of her brow. His fingers touched the pendant hanging from the chain where it rested on her forehead. Suddenly he cried out and stumbled back, holding the hand that had touched the sapphire.

"Galen?"

He looked as if he'd taken a destrier's charge full in the chest. He was breathing hard and cradling his hand. She tried to make him open it, to see what was wrong, but he closed it into a fist so tight she couldn't move it. In any case, he wasn't looking at his hand. He was staring over her head at something. She turned to look, but there wasn't anything there.

Then he began to speak, urgently, as if to someone he could see and she couldn't. "Beware. No, don't. Listen to me. There is danger. Behind you."

"Galen, what ails you?" Honor gripped his arm and tried to get his attention, without success.

Suddenly Galen cried out and sank to one knee, dragging her with him. Honor clutched him or he would have fallen. Uncertain what had come over him, afraid to leave him, she braced her body against his and called his name over and over again. A minute passed, and he gasped. This time his face contorted in an expression of horror.

"Beware!" he cried. "Jennings, look out!"

Frightened, Honor shook him. "Galen, answer me!"

She shook him again, then drew back her hand and slapped him. His head whipped to the side, and when he straightened, the glaze had left his eyes.

He blinked at her. "Honor?" He wet his lips, then he groaned again. "Oh, no."

"You were possessed by something, Galen."

He looked around and noticed they were kneeling on the ground, and groaned. "Damnation and sin." His gaze slid away from hers. "It was a fit. Merely a fit. Had them since I was a boy. Nothing, really. It's gone now. Forget it, I pray you."

Honor planted her hands on her hips and cocked her head to the side while she studied him. He was shaking and too unsteady to rise. He'd sunk back on his heels and wouldn't look at her.

"You said something about Jennings." She thought for a while, then went on. "You acted as if you were seeing something. Galen de Marlowe, you had some kind of vision involving my husband's family, and I have a right to know what it was. You are a sorcerer after all. I have proof of it now.

"I'm *no* sorcerer."

"Then explain yourself."

"I don't have to explain."

He tried to get up, but Honor had to catch him before he fell. She helped him sit, but he tried to get up again. This time she simply pushed him back down.

"Something's happened to you, Galen. Something powerful. You're so weak I can do what I wish with you. Tell me, or I'll go to Isidore Jennings and start asking questions to see if anything's amiss."

Galen clutched her arms and cried, "No! Do you want to destroy me?"

"Of course not. Why would that destroy you?"

"You'll get me accused of witchcraft."

"Everyone knows the de Marlowes have special powers," Honor said.

Galen tightened his grip on her. "Idle talk and rumor are far less dangerous than what you intend to do." He stared into her eyes, and Honor felt so drawn to him she almost forgot what they were talking about.

"My little sunset, you hold my life in your hands."

She gazed into his eyes. They were black in the silver moonlight. She felt him pull her against his chest, and he began to speak quietly. His voice turned her leg bones to water. Even as a child she had been fascinated by Galen de Marlowe. She could be in a pantry, a shed, or a stable and his very presence turned these humble places into magical environs. To him she had always been either a bumbling nuisance or a passing amusement. He had always been the graceful, confident young knight. And now he was asking for her help. The magnificent, imperious Galen needed her.

"Honor, I beg you never to speak of what you just saw. Would you have your troublesome Leekshanks burned at the stake?"

"Burned," she repeated.

How could anyone want to harm Galen, who was so honorable, so valiant? Who would burn such a beautiful man? Then she jolted out of her fixation on his physical charms. Her stomach turned over at the image of Galen tied to a stake, his flesh burning.

"Merciful God in heaven." Without thinking she threw her arms around him and held him in a tight grip. "No. They can't."

"Indeed, they can," he murmured against her hair,

She squeezed him hard. "I'll never speak of it as long as I live. Or after."

Galen managed a smile, which lifted her heart and dispelled the fear she had for him. Suddenly she became aware of how close she was holding him. She released him and moved so that she sat opposite him, glad that it was too dark for him to see her blush.

"Then I can trust you with my life?" he asked.

"Of course. But in return, you must tell me what happened to you."

"I'm not certain." He rubbed his temples. "I don't understand what happened to provoke the vision."

Honor touched the sapphire on her forehead. "You touched this."

He shook his head helplessly.

"You touched it, and moments later you cried out. You spoke the name Jennings. Did you know Aymer gave this chain and pendant to me? It sounded as if you were trying to warn him of something." Honor folded her arms and waited, determined to get an explanation from him.

Galen met her gaze, seemed to read her resolve

and said, "Ah." He sighed and leaned against the stone wall of the well. "Well, then. It seems I must tell you."

Speaking slowly, as if saying the words made him relive a nightmare, Galen said, "There is good reason for my confusion. I—I had a vision of your husband's death."

"Lord protect us," Honor whispered.

"Yes. I never expected such a thing, and we may need His protection if what I saw is true." He rubbed his temples again. "Everything was hazy, but I do remember seeing Aymer riding in the snow beside the Eske. He dismounted on the riverbank. It was muddy, and the sky was filled with black clouds. Aymer was trying to lead his horse down a steep bank when someone wearing a hooded cloak rushed up behind him and clubbed him with a small log. Aymer fell into the river. Everything grew dim after that, but then I glimpsed something strange."

"What was that?"

"A jumble of images: tack in a stable, a storeroom full of spices and herbs, like sage, rosemary, mint, cinnamon, ginger, saffron. Then there was a confusion of things, falcons on their perches, picks and hoes and bricks." Galen pressed his palms against his temples. "A great many bricks, and something about barrels of ale."

"All these things have something to do with Aymer's death?"

"I don't know. I don't understand it. I was so

confused at the last. Mayhap it was the vision disintegrating. But then again, all these things might be important."

"Dear God," Honor said. She felt dazed. Then dread settled over her. "Galen, are these visions always true?"

He closed his eyes. "True? A better description would be that they're always harbingers of things that could be true if I do nothing." He hung his head. "Still I have learned at great cost that following one of them can be more dangerous than not. Damnation sometimes comes either way. But in this case, I'm too late to save Aymer."

In the dark well clearing, silence reigned. Honor felt the slow growth of horror. Who would have wanted to kill Aymer? He'd been a selfish and callous man, but not so evil that he had enemies who thirsted for his blood.

She touched Galen's hand, and he looked up at her. She noticed how unhappy he seemed.

"You don't think I killed him," she said.

"Of course not."

"Then what ails you?"

"Your husband's killer is still free." He moved closer and lowered his voice. "I fear for you, Honor. I will as long as this murderer remains uncaught."

Wetting her dry lips, Honor asked the question she'd been avoiding. "Who did it?"

"I didn't see his face."

"Then what are we going to do?"

Galen rose and helped her stand. "You're going to do nothing. I'll handle this matter myself."

"He was my husband. I want to know what happened to him."

"You loved him."

Honor shook her head. "He never wanted my love." She looked away. "Surely this night's encounter has told you that."

"This night's encounter has made me want— forget this night's encounter," he said, moving away from her.

There it was. His admission that he regretted whatever feelings had led him to make advances. Pain stung her, and Honor swallowed hard. He didn't want her. Not at the price of an honorable arrangement. That was why he no longer wished to remain near her. Even now he was standing at a much greater distance than he had since entering the well clearing.

Honor berated herself for her weakness. This enchanting, beautiful knight, a fabled warrior beloved of kings, wouldn't want her for a wife. She remembered his first wife, Constance. Hair like angels' wings, a sweetness of disposition that Honor could never hope to have. Her death and that of her two children had been a tragedy. Even now, after all these years, Galen still wore a haunted look. Mayhap it was because he was thinking of them. How could plain befreckled Honor Jennings aspire to win the heart of a man who had possessed an angel?

She could not. But that didn't mean she could forget that Aymer had been murdered. That meant that a killer roamed free, and he might still be working evil against others. He must be discovered and punished.

"I'm going to help you find this murderer," she said.

"My little sunset, keep out of it. Don't you realize the danger? You could get killed if the murderer thinks you suspect him. You know nothing of such matters."

Irritated, Honor planted her hands on her hips. "And just how many murderers have you sought, my lord?"

"None, but doing so is too perilous for a woman."

"Aymer wasn't a woman, and he ended up dead."

Galen drew closer again. "I'm not going to argue with you."

"Good. Now, how shall we begin? We were visiting my father when he had the riding accident."

"I have to have time to think, to recall what I can of the vision and decide the best course. You, however, will stay out of this."

She smiled at him. "I'm loath to displease you, my lord, but I don't see that you can stop me."

"You're a stubborn little wretch. I can see I'll have to find this murderer before you get yourself killed. I won't have you meddling."

"Think of this, then." Honor walked away from

him down the flagstone path. "Whoever killed Aymer did it on the Stafford demesne. You'll have to go to Castle Stafford to inquire into the matter. If you want to know who was there and all the other details of the days surrounding his death, you're going to have to ask me. I'm the only one you can ask." She turned to look at him, keeping her voice steady to hide the hurt that threatened to bring tears to her eyes. "I'm the only one you can trust."

Galen was on her in a moment. He gripped her wrist and hissed, "That doesn't mean you should begin asking questions that could get you killed."

Honor pulled free and glared up at him. "I shall be most careful."

"You can't even walk fifty paces without tripping over your gown."

"By my faith, Galen de Marlowe. This vision has made you right evil disposed and snappish."

His voice rose. "I'm not snappish, I'm furious at you."

"I'll not take orders from you, my lord. You're not my husband, and you've no right to give them."

They were almost nose to nose as he ground out, "By the Trinity, in this case might makes right, and if you meddle, I'll thrash you."

Honor jumped out of arm's reach. "That's the most unchivalrous, foul threat I've ever heard."

"Then you're fortunate indeed," Galen said as he closed in on her.

"You stay away from me."

"Come here, my Lady Headstrong."

He lunged and made a grab for her, but Honor dodged aside, whirled around and dashed into the plum trees. She heard him racing after her, but she dared not leave the flagstone path. She might run into a tree and bash her head. So she ran as hard as she could, only to hear his footsteps right behind her just as she reached the garden wall. She cried out when his hand touched her shoulder. She felt her body leave the ground as he lifted her in his arms. She kicked hard, but he dropped one arm so that she landed on her feet. She stumbled, but he caught her and trapped her between his body and the garden wall.

Breathing hard, he wedged a leg between hers and kissed her neck. Just then the garden door swung open. Jacoba and Wilfred stuck their heads out, and Dagobert raced up to her, holding his hat on his head so it wouldn't fall off.

"Ooo, my lady," Wilfred cried.

" 'Ere now, caught you again," Jacoba bellowed. "You stop that, you false, riotous devil."

Galen rounded on them as Dagobert reached Honor. "By the Trinity, be off with you before I toss you all in the holly bushes." He turned to Honor.

Dagobert, still holding his hat on his head, stepped back and delivered a sharp kick to Galen's shin.

"Ouch!" Galen grabbed his leg. "Why, you odious little beast."

He tried to snatch Dagobert, but the boy scrambled around behind Jacoba's ample figure. Jacoba shook her fist at Galen. He groaned and hobbled away from Honor before Jacoba could deliver one of her head-jarring blows. Wilfred grabbed his mistress's hand and pulled her inside the garden while Jacoba stood guard. Dagobert darted into the garden and ran along the path ahead of Wilfred and Honor. Jacoba folded her arms over her ample chest and stood barring Galen's way as Honor was hauled down the path toward the royal hall. Honor looked back over her shoulder and heard Jacoba snort.

"My lady was right to tell me to come for her if she weren't back by midnight. You just keep away from her, my lord, or I'll box your ears till they're big as cabbages."

Honor saw him snarl at the waiting woman, but Jacoba slammed the garden door in his face. Confused and tortured by unfulfilled longings, she allowed Wilfred to pull her back into the hall, into the light and feasting where she was in no danger from Galen de Marlowe.

TWELVE

T HE GARDEN DOOR slammed in Galen's
face. Galen tried the latch, but it was blocked. He
pounded on the door.

"Honor, you come back at once! Honor?"

She was going to do something foolish and expose herself to great peril. He knew it. He hated
that she couldn't see she needed protecting. Fear
for her combined with frustration at not being able
to make her see reason.

Galen rammed his fist against the portal.
"Aargh!"

He cradled his fist and limped back and forth for
a long while, then stopped suddenly as something
else occurred to him. He stared blankly at the curtain of ivy on the garden wall. He had managed to
do something few of his family had done in over

four generations: He'd revealed the secret of his gift to an outsider.

"Bloody damnation and hell."

He shook his aching hand and rubbed his leg while he thought furiously. In spite of having been married, Honor was naive. Eventually she would tell Sir Walter about his vision. Sir Walter, bless him, was a kindly man, but given to distraction. Sooner or later Sir Walter would betray the secret.

Growing cold at the thought, Galen hugged himself and lowered his chin to his chest. Of his brothers, only he had a gift that sometimes took the form of disorienting visions. Usually he had enough warning so that he could isolate himself before the disorientation grew too great. Since the visions were rare, this had not been difficult. But they were coming more frequently of late, and touching that jewel had evoked a vision of such violence that he'd had no time to prepare. Insights inspired by objects were rare for him, although he'd always been sensitive to his surroundings.

Galen winced as he rubbed his leg, then cursed. How could he have known Aymer Jennings had been murdered? Everyone thought he'd drowned. The signs gathered by the men who tried to find him had indicated such a mishap, and the assumption had never been questioned. But now he knew the truth.

Equally as important was how to keep Honor from revealing his secret. She wouldn't mean to do him harm, but she was such a bundle of impetuousness and calamity. Galen straightened, working his bruised fingers as he faced the truth. The de Marlowes had ways of dealing with accidental exposures such as this. Enemies who learned the secret were eliminated. In this generation there had been few such. His brother Simon had been forced to kill one in self-defense.

Honor was no enemy, and she was a woman. Marriage was the only way to ensure a woman's silence. Many generations of his mother's family had employed it. It was how his mother had married his father. Once an outsider became a member of the family, he or she shared the risks that came with these special gifts. Not every child possessed a gift, but his mother's five sons had all inherited it.

Galen had always expected one of his feckless younger brothers to be the one to get himself into trouble this way. Simon would be furious. Macaire would laugh at him. Fabron would smile at him knowingly. And Fulk? Fulk would keep his distance, his dignified, polite distance. But they would all know, and he wouldn't blame them for resenting this risk he'd forced upon them.

"Blessed God, forgive me," he muttered. "What else can I do?"

He would have to marry Honor Jennings. He had to keep a tight rein on her impetuous tongue. No one could do that but a husband. She might well become even angrier once she had time to fully realize how shabbily Aymer, the arse, had treated her regarding marital intimacy. She might blame Galen for forcing her to see the truth.

People who had been hurt often struck out at the nearest target, regardless of culpability. He'd seen Honor when she was in a rage; she might blurt out anything if angry enough. But if she were his wife, she'd be subject to him. She would have to keep any secret he wished her to keep, and she would want to protect any children they had.

Pressing the palms of his hands against his eyes, Galen fought the jolt of fear caused by the thought of marriage. A vicious black whirlwind of terror scourged his heart. He braced his legs apart, pressed his hands against the ivy clinging to the wall and fought the onslaught. Panting, tortured and furious with himself, he remained there in the darkness until at last he mastered himself. Slowly he stood erect, fumbled with the short cloak that hung from one shoulder, and tried the door latch again. This time it opened easily. Had it ever been blocked?

Once in the royal garden, Galen hurried back to the hall, where the banquet was winding down. Music sounded from the minstrel gallery, and soon dancing would begin. Galen didn't see Honor at first, but then he spotted Sir Walter's silver head bobbing and shaking in the midst of a group of noblemen. At the edge of this group he glimpsed the edge of a blue gown embroidered with gold stars. Honor.

Galen shouldered his way through the crowds to the corner of the hall where Honor and her father were. As he approached, he recognized the men around Sir Walter. Isidore Jennings, Lord Andrew Swan, and Sir Lionel Titchwell had backed the older man into a corner, and lurking at the edge of the group, casting a lascivious eye at Honor, was Drogo Scattergood. Galen could see the spittle at the corners of the man's mouth from where he stood.

"De Marlowe."

Galen started out of his concentration and bowed to the king, who was making a progress around the hall with the queen on his arm. Edward waved a hand at the courtiers around him. They stepped back, and the king summoned Galen to him and lowered his voice.

"Hark you that brawl simmering in the corner over there?"

"You mean that pack of dogs around Sir Walter Stafford, Sire?"

"Aye, of course you've noticed. I'll not have a scene at my banquet. Do you understand?" Edward cast a wary glance at his brother, the Duke of Clarence. "I see my dear brother is exchanging pleasantries with King Louis' ambassador. No doubt he's asking for a few thousand men with which to topple me from my throne." The king glanced back at Sir Walter. "This is no time for a feud among that many powerful barons, de Marlowe.

Find a solution and employ it at once. You have my permission. Get the girl married and her lands safely disposed of."

"But, majesty, I—" Galen's heart was pounding so hard he was sure the king must hear it. He forced the words out. "Sire, I wish to ally myself to Sir Walter."

"What? God's teeth, you make a jest."

Queen Elizabeth joined them. "A jest, your highness?"

Edward gave a loud bark of a laugh and took the queen's hand. "A mighty jest indeed, de Marlowe. Bess, my sweet, do you know what de Marlowe just said? He said he wished to marry little Honor Jennings. It hasn't been many hours since he begged me to match her with anyone who could get her away from him."

The queen turned her golden head in Galen's direction. Galen bowed low to cover the fact that his face was scarlet. When he straightened, he found himself under the scrutiny of a pair of calculating green eyes.

"Sire," the queen said. "If Lord de Marlowe has spoken of an alliance after years of avoiding one . . ."

The king was already studying Galen. Galen looked at his boots and prayed no one else had heard the king's remarks.

"Come here, de Marlowe."

Galen knelt before the king.

"It's as I thought, is it not?"

"Sire?"

"You're in love with the girl."

Galen pressed his lips together. "The alliance is a good one for both families. Does Your Highness not wish for the union between two loyal families?"

"I've nothing against the match, Galen, except that I could reward your service to me with a far richer prize than Honor Jennings."

"To me, Sire, there is no more valuable prize."

King Edward put a hand on Galen's shoulder. "Are you certain, my friend?" He nodded toward the men surrounding Sir Walter. "You'll make powerful enemies if you take her away from that lot."

Galen felt cold and hot at the same time. He nodded. "Yes, Sire, I'm certain."

"Very well. You have my permission, and you may speak to Sir Walter." The king offered his arm to the queen. "And do it quickly, before Jennings or one of the others causes trouble."

Galen rose and inclined his head. "Yes, Sire."

The queen passed by him and gave him a sly smile. "I had not thought to find in you such perception in your choice of a new wife, Lord de Marlowe. God grant you much happiness."

"Your Highness," Galen murmured.

He kept his head lowered until the king and queen passed, then he walked swiftly the rest of the way across the hall to the cornered Sir Walter Stafford.

"Peace, good gentles," Sir Walter was saying. "I have but one daughter, and she can't marry all of you."

"I have a right to be consulted," Isidore Jennings said. "She obviously has renounced her vows, never meant to keep them. I shall be much offended if Drogo Scattergood is not the man."

Sir Lionel Titchwell snarled at Jennings. "Hold your tongue. I was the first to offer for her."

"No, I was," said Andrew Swan.

Sir Walter looked from one man to the other uneasily.

Honor stood on tiptoe to see over his shoulder. "I've told you over and over, Sir Lionel. I remain true to my vows."

"Ha!"

Isidore ignored her. "I demand the right to put forth an offer, Stafford. Are you going to give me offense?"

Galen spoke up. "You're giving me offense, Jennings."

"Not you again," Isidore growled.

"What has he to do with this?" Drogo Scattergood asked in his whining voice.

"I, good sirs, am the only suitor among you with the king's blessing," Galen said.

All the men gaped at him, and Honor peered around her father's shoulder, her blue eyes round. "*What?*"

"Being the king's favorite doesn't give you the right to interfere in privy matters," Jennings snapped. "Go away, de Marlowe. I'm about to arrange a match between my cousin Scattergood and Lady Honor."

Aware that Honor was gaping at him as if he'd suddenly sprouted horns and a forked tail, Galen shouldered Andrew Swan aside and joined Sir Walter. "Now, making such an arrangement would be offensive indeed since I've just come to offer for Lady Honor myself, and as I said, with the king's blessing."

Silence spread from the center of the group outward. Several people who had been watching the exchange stirred. Then the whispering began and rippled through the court. Galen paid it no heed, but he glanced at Honor, willing her to keep silent. Foolish wish.

"But I'm a vowess," she cried. "What fresh trickery is this?"

"Hush, daughter," Sir Walter said. He eyed Galen for a long moment, then nodded.

"Father!"

Sir Walter turned on Honor. "Be silent, or leave. That is my last word to you." Honor's mouth snapped shut, and she gave Galen a glance of confused horror.

Galen looked at Sir Walter with new respect. When the need was urgent, he could be firm.

"I welcome your offer, de Marlowe." He glanced at the noblemen surrounding them.

Galen joined him in staring and allowed his hand to drift to the hilt of his sword. No one was going to fight in the royal hall, but the implication was clear. Anyone who challenged him was taking a grave risk. Jennings, Scattergood, and the rest retreated. This at least was one advantage. He would be able to protect her now. When the men were gone Honor slipped around her father and confronted him.

Hissing in a low voice, she said, "By the saints, what madness is this?"

"Smile, Honor. The whole court is watching."

Her lips stretched into a semblance of a smile. "What are you doing?"

Sir Walter stepped between them and took his daughter's hand. He placed it in Galen's and covered Galen's hand with his.

"This isn't unexpected, de Marlowe. I began to suspect you had it in mind the moment you offered to help me find Honor a husband, back at Castle Stafford."

"You did?" Galen asked faintly.

Sir Walter leaned close. "I saw you with her through the window while I was talking to the gardener. I vow I never beheld two more enamored young people in my life. Of course, we must negotiate. You'll do right by my daughter or you'll not have her, mark my words." Sir Walter turned to answer inquiries from several friends.

Honor was looking at Galen differently now. He didn't understand why she was staring at him with such a wondrous expression.

"Is it true?"

"Is what true?"

She looked around to make sure they weren't overheard. "What my father said. Is it true? Were you but pretending to help Father make an alliance when all along you intended to make an offer yourself?"

Galen opened his mouth, then closed it. Whatever he said would be wrong. To say yes was a lie; to say no would greatly offend her. His guilt was growing by the minute. He knew she desired him, but she also spent most of her time angry with him. The whole situation was a disaster. At least there was something he could tell her that was true.

"Honor, I have already shown you many testaments to my desire for you." He should tell her immediately that this, like any other marriage among people of their rank, was essentially an alliance. It was the right thing to do. His other reason must be revealed when they were safely alone. He was going to explain, then her eyes began to shine.

"Oh, Galen."

His mouth had opened, but the words he'd planned died on his lips when he heard those two words. She said them like a prayer, a prayer that had been answered. To his everlasting shame, he said nothing when her hand moved, with hesitation and timidity. Slowly it reached out, hung there before him, a small peace offering. No, more than a peace offering. Galen suddenly understood as he looked into those eyes, those shining, love-struck eyes. Honor Jennings was offering her heart.

Mute with self-loathing, Galen took her hand and brushed it with his lips.

Honor drew close. "I didn't know. You were as confused as I. Neither of us could admit what we felt, but you're wiser. You discovered the truth first. Was it in the plum orchard? Of course it was. I ask foolish questions, and I'm babbling."

She squeezed his hand and looked up at him with an open admiration that made him want to howl with frustration.

"I will do everything in my power to be a good wife," she said. Biting her lip, she continued. "You were kind to praise me in the orchard, but I know I have faults. We both do, but we can improve together." She smiled up at him shyly. "I'll even admit I can be quite stubborn. There, I've said it."

"Oh, Honor, don't." He was growing more miserable by the moment. He dropped her hand. "You'll do excellent well the way you are." He looked away from her glowing face. "I must go."

"Why?"

He thought quickly. "The king. I must speak with the king, and my family too. You don't know what my brothers are like."

"And then you'll return."

He was already backing away. "Not tonight. Tomorrow. Tell your father I will call tomorrow."

"Galen, don't go."

"Duty, Honor. The king is waiting."

He rushed from her as if hellhounds were after him. He lost himself in the crowds of courtiers, then left the hall without looking back. He didn't want to see her bewilderment, her disappointment. And if he saw hurt in her eyes, he didn't think he could bear it.

"God forgive me. What have I done?"

THIRTEEN

THE MORNING AFTER the royal banquet saw Honor ensconced on a cushion in the queen's solar. Dazed, uncertain but ecstatic at the same time, she hardly cared that she'd been accorded the honor of attending Her Highness. Queen Elizabeth was reading from a stack of letters while her ladies embroidered, read, and listened to a minstrel playing on his lute. Honor pretended to listen to the music, but she was really trying to adjust to the idea that Galen de Marlowe had asked for her hand.

She hadn't slept all night. Her mind flitted from one thought to another. First she thought of how detestably Galen had acted toward her, then she remembered his sweet smile and gentle hands, but soon she began to worry.

She was certain Galen was as confused as she. Why else would he behave in so contradictory a manner. He'd been so stubborn and hateful about Durance Guarde. Honor smiled. But, now that she thought of it, he'd never really objected to her personally.

"What are you smirking about, Lady Honor?"

Jolted out of her reverie, Honor looked up at Lady Nicolette, the blonde who had simpered at Galen last night. Nicolette had been eyeing her hatefully ever since Honor came into the solar. She glanced over her shoulder at the queen, who was still reading letters, then hissed at Honor.

"Stupid girl. Galen simply wants Castle Stafford and its lands. It's unseemly for you to moon about the palace as if you were a beautiful princess who'd won the love of a king."

Honor cocked her head to the side. "I pray you, Lady Nicolette, if what you say is true, why then did he not ask for your hand? Your dowry is twice the size of mine."

Nicolette boiled like a laundry cauldron.

"I'm merely curious," Honor said calmly.

Behind her two of the queen's ladies giggled. Nicolette glared at them, stalked over to a window and pretended to look at the view.

Honor returned to her puzzlement. She had done this all night to no avail, but early in the morning it occurred to her that his gift must have played a role. Mayhap Galen, having seen her so much, finally had a vision of them together.

He denied working spells on her, and she believed him. A man who had a gift such as his had no need of other magic. God had blessed him. What wonders must he have seen. And horrors, she thought, remembering what Galen had said about Aymer's death.

A shadow passed over her happiness. Poor Aymer had been murdered. By whom? She and Galen must find out. He was right; Aymer's killer must be brought to justice. They must find him before they married. She didn't want this horrible mystery hanging over their life together.

Honor smiled. Who would have thought old Leekshanks, the scourge of Durance Guarde, would want to marry her? He could have anyone. He could have the beautiful and rich Nicolette, although he had better taste than to chose her.

She admired his reputation as a fierce yet honorable warrior and as a loyal friend to the king. And to conduct himself with such integrity in spite of having so powerful a talent—that was honor indeed. He could have used the power of his visions for personal gain, but he never had. Many noblemen had curried favor with the king and been rewarded handsomely. Galen took little and aspired to even less.

But he was right to keep the visions a secret. Many would fear it. Some would try to use him. Still others would try to destroy him. Yet he'd trusted her with his secret. Honor blushed and glanced around the solar, hoping no one saw her. He must love her greatly to trust her with so dangerous a secret, and she would protect it and him with her life.

Honor stirred on her cushion. She was growing bored. Galen was closeted with the king, her father, and law clerks. She sighed and propped her chin on her fist. Marriage was a complicated matter when there were lands and titles involved. Her first marriage contract had taken a whole day to arrange.

"Lady Honor." It was one of the queen's younger ladies, a small, dark-haired girl named Marie.

"Yes, Lady Marie."

Marie dropped onto a cushion beside her, and another lady joined them. Lady Marie whispered behind her hand.

"Pray you, what is he like?"

The other girl giggled and nodded. "Yes, what's he like?"

"Who?"

"Lord de Marlowe, of course."

"Oh." Honor was taken aback. No one had ever wanted to know what Aymer was like. Then her spirits lifted. "Why, he's a perfect gentle knight."

"Yes," Lady Marie said as she leaned closer and lowered her voice even more. "But his kiss. Is it as magical as they say? They say he's dark, dangerous, and sinister. Is his kiss dark, dangerous, and sinister?"

Honor's jaw dropped. Luckily she was saved

from answering when the queen clapped her hands.

"Stop that giggling and whispering, Marie. Honor is not going to discuss her betrothed's personal qualities with you. Nor will I have such wanton conduct in my household."

Honor sighed and picked up a piece of cloth from the sewing basket at her side. Attending a queen was proving to be a most tedious duty. She had things to do. She wanted to visit the Westminster tilers and engage them to tile the floors of the house she was still going to build at Durance Guarde. She had to reengage the master mason and his crew and talk to her architect. Still, all that must wait if she was to be married.

Glancing at Nicolette, Honor was careful not to allow herself to smile and be accused of smirking again. But she couldn't help smiling. Especially when she thought of Galen, his long legs and slim hips, strong thighs and hot mouth. Oh, dear. Now she was flushed. Honor ducked her head, pretending to examine a stitch. This was going to be a long, long day.

TO HONOR'S DISMAY it took three whole days to arrange a marriage contract. During that time Galen tried to seek her out, but the queen proved a most vigilant guardian. On the fourth day Honor was in the London lodgings taken by Sir Walter for their stay, fidgeting while Jacoba fastened her into a gown of emerald silk.

"Hurry," she said. "He'll be here soon."

"Just you be still and let me put this veil on your head."

"I don't need a veil."

"It's not proper to go about London town without covering your hair. Put this circlet on to hold it in place. By my faith, it's a wonder you attracted Lord de Marlowe's interest, what with you refusing to shave your forehead to make your brow appear high and never wearing a proper headdress nor nothing."

"I'll not shave my forehead, Jacoba. It's absurd. Did you see Lady Marie? She's shaved her forehead and her eyebrows. Her head looks like a boiled egg."

"It's the fashion."

"Fashion be damned." Honor scuttled out of Jacoba's reach and flew to the window. "He's here. Where's my cloak? Where's my cloak?"

Honor grabbed the garment from Jacoba, but the waiting woman held her back.

"Now, you wait, my fine lady. You walk down them stairs without haste, as befits your father's daughter. Else you're sure to fall down them."

"But—"

"Remember yesterday. You fell the last two steps because you won't look where you're going."

"Oh, very well. I'll walk slowly."

She left her room and would have bolted down the dark wooden staircase, but Jacoba collared Dagobert and pushed him in front of her mistress.

"Just you go ahead, boy, and be dignified about it."

Dagobert straightened his tunic huffily at the implied insult, settled his cap on his head, and preceded Honor with a stately march. Hemmed in by Jacoba and the page, Honor had no choice but to walk rather than run. By the time she reached the hall, an alarming timidity stole over her.

She hadn't been alone with Galen since the night of the banquet. Yesterday in the royal garden he'd tried to pull her through the door that led to the plum orchard, but the queen saw him and called Honor to her. Her Highness was one of the few people in the world who could thwart Galen successfully.

Now he was here, dressed in dark-brown velvet and soft riding boots, filling the hall with his tall elegance and that air of mystery that so captivated women. Now she understood it. The reserve, the guardedness was a part of him.

He was like some jeweled treasure chest shrouded in darkness. You could see the gleam of costly metal and stone, glimpse ornate carving, sense the treasures locked inside. Although you might long for him, you couldn't touch. He wouldn't let you. And the more he refused, the more you longed to touch, to possess. Lady Marie had begged her to cut a lock of that silky dark hair as a treasure. Honor had replied that she wouldn't dare.

"Honor, don't just hover by the stair," Sir Walter said. "Lord de Marlowe is waiting."

Honor came forward, twisting her cloak in her hands, uncertain.

Then Galen said, "Don't scold her, I pray you. She has good reason to hesitate after the many times I was so inhospitable at Durance Guarde."

"You were a saint to endure her plaguing you," Sir Walter replied with a chuckle as he took Honor's hand. "But it's all ended marvelous well." He placed her hand in Galen's. "Be of good cheer, daughter, for we've signed at least a hundred documents put before us by clerks, and the betrothal ceremony will take place at Castle Stafford in less than a fortnight."

Honor hardly paid her father any attention. She couldn't take her eyes from Galen, and his gaze never left her. Then he seemed to wake from some intense meditation.

"We must be off, Sir Walter. The king's favorite goldsmith will wait upon us, and we must ride all the way to St. Paul's and down Cheapside."

Galen placed Honor's hand on his arm and guided her out of the house. In the street his man Ralph waited, holding Galen's horse and Honor's mare. Galen turned to her and kissed her hand.

"Honor, my sweet, I must speak to you privily. It's terribly important, and I can't wait much longer."

Honor nodded, smiling happily at the idea that he longed to be alone with her as she did with him. Then he scowled at something over her shoulder.

"Oh, no."

Honor turned and saw Jacoba plodding around the corner of the town house on a donkey.

"Send her away," Galen said.

Jacoba pulled up beside them and handed Honor her riding gloves. "You'll not take my mistress anywhere without me. Sir Walter's orders, me lord. So just you trot along, and be on your best chivalrous behavior."

"Jacoba!" Honor cried. She heard Ralph snigger, and she cast an apologetic look at Galen.

Pressing his lips together, Galen conducted Honor to her horse and helped her mount. Their little procession wound through the streets of London. Cobbled, narrow, filled with pedestrians, they were hemmed in on either side by houses and shops. They rounded St. Paul's with its towering spires and worked their way down the long street called Cheapside. It was here that most of the goldsmiths of London had their workshops.

Galen stopped at a large building faced with carved stone and helped Honor dismount. Her ears filled with the banging and tapping that issued from the rear of the shop. Not far away she saw a tavern, and next to the goldsmith's shop was a moneychanger's establishment where two men were weighing gold coins at the shop front.

Not waiting for Jacoba to dismount, Galen offered his arm to Honor and conducted her inside. As they entered, a man dressed in a rich damask robe embroidered with gold thread came to meet them. Bowing gracefully, he greeted Galen in a quiet voice filled with authority and assurance.

"My lord, this is a pleasure."

Galen nodded, and spoke to Honor. "I must have a word with Master Shaa."

An assistant offered Honor a seat in front of a table covered in black velvet. With flourishing gestures and a confident smile, he began to unveil objects. First he produced a chalice of fluted agate on a flared gold base. Graceful handles curved up the sides of the vessel, and the filigree was adorned with cabochon rubies. Honor smiled and murmured her admiration, but was distracted when she heard Jacoba enter. Before the waiting woman could join her mistress Master Shaa intercepted her, holding forth a delicate silver chain from which dangled an enameled pendant. Jacoba's eyes grew as big as cherries.

"Honor," Galen said.

She hadn't even seen him approach. "Galen, why am I looking at these vessels?"

"Wedding gifts," he said.

"But I don't need—"

"If you please, I would speak to you while your dragon of a maid is occupied."

He glanced at Jacoba, who was standing before a mirror wearing the silver chain. Galen held out his hand. Honor took it, and she rose. The smiling assistant held back a curtain behind a counter, and Galen led her into a room. There she beheld walls filled with shelves, and on the shelves rested metal objects too numerous to count—mazers, cruets, reliquaries, caskets, chalices. Honor noticed a set of silver book covers decorated with scenes from the Bible. Around the room were several heavy chests bound with iron and enormous locks, but, in truth, she had little interest in the room. Galen had been trying to speak to her for days, and she thought she knew why.

Galen picked up a small box with a peaked lid engraved with traceried arches. He opened and closed the lid while Honor watched. His brow furrowed.

"Honor, when we're not quarreling about Durance Guarde, you and I deal well together, do we not?"

Staring at the tips of her boots, Honor said, "Up to now, when we weren't quarreling we were—I mean, you . . ."

"Ah, yes. My unchivalrous conduct." Suddenly Galen slammed the box down on the table. "Damnation and sin, this is cursed difficult."

"I don't understand." She did, but she desperately wanted to hear what he was attempting to say.

Galen threw up his hands and uttered a wordless sound of frustration. He gripped the edge of the table and scowled at the golden box as if he dared not look at her. Mayhap she should try to put him at ease. She went to him and touched his sleeve. He turned his head aside, but she spoke anyway.

"Galen, if we're to marry, we can build my house at Durance Guarde together, could we not?"

"What? Oh, yes."

"I have such plans." Honor grew excited as she spoke. "I wish you could see the marvels I want to bring there. Such painting, such sculpture. Oh, Galen, we could go to Florence after the wedding. We could share this task I've set myself." He was looking at her oddly.

"What's wrong?" she asked.

"Nothing, my little sunset. Your eyes light with rapture when you speak of your art treasures and grand building schemes. I've seen Florence and Venice. You're right. There is a new light spreading over the world now that the scholars have discovered so much learning from ancient Rome and Greece." He touched her cheek. "You have absorbed this rebirth into your soul, and that, my love, is already unique."

Wonder spread through Honor, making her tingle and stealing her breath. He had called her *love*.

She moved closer to him; her eyes fastened on his mouth, those soft lips that had taught her more in one kiss than she'd learned in her whole life with Aymer. Her lips almost touched his.

He groaned and let her kiss him, then abruptly drew back. "No!"

She opened her mouth, but he set her from him. "No, Honor. Don't touch me, or I'll never be able to say this. We don't have much time before Jacoba remembers her duty, and I have two important things to say to you. First, I must follow this vision of Aymer's murder when I come to Castle Stafford for the wedding."

"I know that."

"I like it not that a killer might still roam your father's demesne."

Honor smiled, then laughed and threw herself into Galen's arms.

Frowning, Galen caught her and said, "There's nothing amusing about this, Honor."

"No," she said, raising on tiptoe to put her arms around his neck. She looked into his eyes. "No, there isn't, but I love it that you worry about me. I—I love you, Galen."

"Honor, don't."

"I know you're supposed to fall to your knees and make all sorts of dramatic vows, and such, but I had to say it after you'd given me so many proofs of your love. By my faith, Galen, I never thought to find you shy, but you've been trying to confess your love for four days now. I had to help."

"Oh, dear God in heaven," Galen said.

She grinned at him, but he was looking over her head, an expression of grim dread on his face. She turned in his arms to find three men, all with silky dark hair and that lean de Marlowe stature that reminded her of tall birch trees. One of them sauntered over to them.

"God in heaven, Simon," Galen said.

"Aye, dear brother. God in heaven, what have you done now?"

FOURTEEN

DRESSED IN ONE of his most elaborate tunics of red and gold damask, Galen rode down the path that wound through the forest past Durance Guarde. He was on his way to Castle Stafford, and on either side of him rode his brothers Simon and Macaire. Fulk and Fabron rode behind. Outriders trotted ahead, and behind came men-at-arms and guarded wagons laden with gifts for his betrothed. Macaire was whistling, while Simon stared ahead. Fabron was talking quietly to his twin with a grim expression on his face.

The whistling stopped, and Macaire glanced at Galen. "He's still not speaking to us."

"You can't blame him," Fabron said lightly. "After all, we did burst in upon him and prevent his confession."

"By the blessed Trinity," Simon replied. "That's no reason to be so stubborn." He cast a fulminating glance at his older brother. "You have to tell us. We already know you've had a vision full of dark portent, probably more than one."

Galen merely turned and glared at Fulk. His quiet, shy brother was the only one who could know such an intimate detail. Fulk flushed and looked away.

Macaire was whistling again. He leaned over and slapped Galen on the arm. "Come now, you have to tell us sometime. Begin with the little Jennings creature. We're desperate to know what possessed you after all these years to make an offer, and for such a fey little thing."

Galen scowled, but he couldn't remain furious with Macaire for long. Macaire simply ignored his ill humor and carried on as if everything were well between them. Faced with such determined good humor, it was impossible to remain angry. He sighed.

"It wasn't that she's tempting, although the Lord knows she is." Galen shook his head helplessly. "It was that she's both tempting and—and fatally endearing. From the moment she crashed through the door at Durance Guarde she . . ."

Galen leaned on his saddle pommel and tried to make sense of what had happened to him. "I don't know. It's as if she infected me. Perhaps she became a shade and entered my body, and now she's with me all the time."

He noticed that both Simon and Macaire were staring at him. He turned and saw that the twins were looking at him as if he were crazed.

"You don't understand," he snapped. "How could you. None of you has ever been in—"

"Love," Fulk finished for him.

Galen twisted around and hissed, "Damnation and sin, Fulk. Will you stay out of my mind please? God deliver me from your cursed invasions."

"I'm not trying to hear your thoughts," Fulk replied. "You're shouting them."

"I care not." Simon pulled up his horse, and the whole procession stopped, with the attendants keeping their distance. "You swore an oath on Mother's grave, as did we all, never to expose the family by revealing the secret. This isn't like you, Galen. You have to tell us what's wrong."

Galen stared at his most severe brother and finally relented. "I couldn't prevent what happened. I had a vision while we were together. She already knows part of the secret."

"I knew it!" Simon cried. "I knew there had to be some grave reason for this madness. You're marrying her to keep her silent. You could have admitted it, you know."

Macaire said, "Leave off, Simon. Galen is much troubled and needs time."

"Well, he hasn't got time, has he? He's on his way to his betrothal, and in a fortnight he's going to marry that snip of a girl who has no sense and less grace."

Galen rounded on Simon. "She has sense. She's extremely clever. More clever than you, dear brother. I'd match her wits against any don at Oxford, and she inquires into everything. Architecture, philosophy, printing." Galen smiled, forgetting his irritating brother. "And she has eyes that contain all the shades of blue from azure to indigo."

"Oh, well, that explains it, then, by my troth. The next time I take a fancy to a blue-eyed wench I'll just tell her everything, shall I?"

"Use that word to refer to her again, and I'll nail your ears back," Galen snapped.

Macaire protested as the two oldest brothers glared at each other. Fulk and Fabron whispered together, then Fulk nudged his horse between Simon and Galen.

Fabron rode up beside Macaire, unfazed by the violent emotions blazing between the elder brothers. "Listen, Galen wants to tell Honor the secret before he marries her." He caught Simon's irate gaze and lifted an eyebrow. "There's more to this than any of us suspected. More peril than he's willing to admit."

It was as if a chill passed from brother to brother. Galen felt it, felt their eyes upon him. So far he'd resisted telling them about the Tower vision. Telling them exposed them to great danger, but now he realized they'd never let him keep it from them. With the twins around, it would be impossible anyway. Fabron sensed his emotions, and Fulk, if he tried, could read his thoughts like a book of hours. That was one of the primary reasons why he'd isolated himself at Durance Guarde in the first place.

Macaire was the first to throw off the feeling of dread. "I don't care what you say. Galen would never endanger us."

Fulk turned his horse so that he faced Galen. He held Galen's eyes with his. The others waited quietly, knowing better than to interrupt the silent intercourse. Then Fulk spoke for the first time.

"The vision came when he touched her."

"But, I don't understand," said Simon. "That's never happened before."

"It wasn't simply that I touched her. I touched a stone Aymer Jennings gave her, and glimpsed his murder."

"She murdered him?" Macaire exclaimed.

"No, you fool."

"The question is," said Simon, leaning in Galen's direction. "Are you out of control because of this woman?"

"No! Now leave me alone."

Fabron put his hand on Simon's arm. "Yes, leave him. He doesn't want to speak of it. He's confused about the girl, and about something else far darker."

"I want to know what that is, damn it," Simon said. "I want to know what's wrong."

Fabron smiled. "Oh, Simon. You're so bullheaded. It doesn't matter what you want if Galen can't bring himself to confide in us yet." With this, he kicked his horse into a trot and rode off. The outriders moved on. After a whispered conversation, Fulk, Macaire, and Simon left. Galen guided his horse off the path and watched the other men ride by, then the wagons. At last he was alone with his dread and his guilt.

He was on his way to betroth himself to Honor. He would remain at Castle Stafford until he married her. During that time he had to find out the truth behind Aymer Jennings' disappearance, but it looked as if his brothers would do everything in their power to prevent him from telling Honor why they had to marry. Yet he didn't think he could bring himself to deceive her. He wished he knew what to do.

"You're right."

Galen jumped and wheeled his horse around to find Fulk riding toward him through the forest.

"It's frightening to expose oneself to another." Fulk looked at his older brother gravely. He had their father's pale blue eyes, ones so pale the pupils stood out like obsidian against silver.

"Why is it that the quietest, shyest, most retiring of my brothers is the most frightening?" Galen asked.

"I'm not trying to frighten you."

"But you know."

Fulk nodded. "Don't tell her about the Tower vision. It has nothing to do with her or the vision of Aymer's death. But she's determined to discover what happened to Jennings, and I don't think you'll be able to stop her. If you reveal the other to her, she might imperil all of us."

"Christ, Fulk. Don't you think I know that?" Galen grabbed his brother's arm and hauled him close. "I didn't want you to know about the Tower vision, damn you. Not *you*." He ruffled Fulk's hair and released him.

"You should be grateful for my aid."

"Knowing about the Tower vision places you in terrible danger," Galen said softly. "But since it can't be helped, I'll be grateful if you keep Simon from interfering between Honor and me."

Fulk asked, "Does she love you enough to keep the secret?"

Galen nodded.

"But you're not certain of your feelings for her."

His thoughts veered to Constance and his children. "I never wanted this. Honor is too precious to risk."

"And you see great risk in times to come," Fulk said.

"I think so, but not for years yet." Galen shook his head. "Fear not, Honor lives up to her name. She would never betray me, never lie to me, which is more than I can say for myself."

"Galen," Fulk said gently, "Simon is right. Say nothing to her until after the wedding. Please, I beg you."

Galen scowled at his brother. "They sent you back apurpose, didn't they?"

"No." Fulk appeared to steel himself for something and spoke again. "I came back without their urging. I beg you, Galen, protect yourself. You have but to wait a short time, and then you can tell her everything you wish."

"I can't."

"Yes, you can." Fulk pressed his lips together. "Simon told me to tell you he thinks Honor may be in danger once you begin to hunt for Aymer's murderer. There's enough at risk as it is. Do you want to expose her to more peril?"

Galen stared into his brother's eyes, eyes that had never lied to him. Fulk's gift was perhaps the most powerful of all his brothers. He could share thoughts with another so intimately that he almost became the other person. He could do this without having to see or touch the one with whom he wished to share. It was the very magnitude of his power that caused him to retreat from others, for the gift was as invasive as a knife in the heart. As a child Fulk had often been terrified at what he saw in the minds of others. For many years Galen and Simon had taken turns guarding him, watching out for him until he grew old enough to protect himself. As time passed he learned to shield himself from the thoughts of others and seldom let down his guard except when he was alone with his family. He was smiling sadly at Galen now.

"Just find Jennings' killer, marry Honor, and then tell her the truth. You'll see. All will be well."

"I—I'll think about it."

They began to ride, and Fulk gave Galen another of his rare smiles. The path left the forest, and over the hilltops they could see the Stafford pennant flying from the highest tower of the castle.

"You can always take Macaire's advice," Fulk said as they stared at the waving pennant. "He said to wed her, bed her, then talk to her. He said that if she balks, you can always lock her up in Durance Guarde until she gets over her fury."

"All that proves, my dear Fulk, is that Macaire doesn't know Honor Jennings at all."

FIFTEEN

UNTIL GALEN DE MARLOWE rode across the drawbridge of Castle Stafford, Honor had almost convinced herself that she'd dreamed that he'd asked for her hand. Either that or he was even more wicked than she'd once assumed and he wouldn't appear at all, leaving her to endure the shame of being publicly rejected.

But two days ago he'd come riding into her life again, more handsome than the costly raiment he wore, more possessed of mysterious charm, and more exquisitely enticing than her imagination had remembered. Upon his arrival, all he had to do was swing one of those long legs down from his horse and walk over to her, the muscles working beneath the fine hose, and she was flustered, awkward, and mute.

Luckily his brothers had surrounded them, and no one could remain flustered under the attention of four courtly young men bent on admiration and chivalry. They laughed, joked, and teased her. All except Fulk, who seemed to have been appointed Galen's guardian. He remained at his brother's side constantly and watched Honor with a grave yet benign regard that provoked her curiosity.

With five such virile and active young men about the place, Castle Stafford hummed with activity. Soon more relatives would arrive for the betrothal ceremony, but at the moment Honor had Galen to herself for the first time since his arrival, almost. It was after noontide and Master Baldwin Trune, the steward, was giving them a tour of the castle from the vantage point of the wall walk.

To Honor one castle was much like the next, but Master Baldwin was anxious to display the great fortress that was under his care, and she must be patient. So she walked beside Galen with her hand on his arm, while Baldwin described crop yields and the extent of the forests and pointed out the dovecote and the piggery.

"You will notice, my lord, that our kitchen is of stone," Baldwin said as he gestured toward the elaborate building with its steeple and brewhouse.

"An excellent innovation," Galen murmured.

Baldwin brightened. "I have yet to show you the smithy, the stables, and the wagon shed. This way, my lord."

On they trod, with Baldwin in the lead. Jacoba and Dagobert trailed them at a distance.

Galen leaned down and whispered, "Would God I'd accepted your father's invitation to hunt as my brothers did."

"I'm sorry," Honor said. "But Master Baldwin has always taken great pride in Castle Stafford. He makes improvements and repairs every winter. I think it takes his mind from his daughter." Honor glanced behind them to make sure Dagobert was out of earshot. "My page's mother was his daughter, and she died when she was quite young."

Galen looked at Dagobert. He seemed ready to make a comment, but then appeared to change his mind. "May God rest her soul." They listened to Baldwin detail the wonders of the smithy, but when he passed through a tower on his way to the wagon shed, Galen held her back.

"Honor, my patience is running out, and so is time. I've met every retainer and servant in the entire place: Jacoba, Wilfred, Perkin the gardener, that little barbarian Dagobert, the bailiffs and reeves, the huntsman and falconer, even the cook. We're never alone, and I must hear the tale of Aymer's death from you."

"I know," Honor said, distracted by the severity of his expression. He seemed all the more entrancing when he was serious. "Tonight we could meet after compline. My father and your brothers will be tired from hunting, and everyone will be asleep."

They stepped out of the tower and onto the wall where Baldwin had paused to wait for them. Honor pointed at one of the towers across the bailey.

"We could meet in the mill tower."

"Honor, my sweet, the towers will be patrolled."

She grinned. "They won't patrol the piggery."

He gave her a long-suffering look as they walked along the battlements.

She pointed down toward the stables. "How about the haystacks?"

He stopped and looked at her.

"Do you make a jest?"

Her brow wrinkled. "No. Why?"

"God's teeth."

"What's wrong?"

"Oh, nothing." He smiled at Baldwin and motioned for him to continue to lead the way. "I never did like your husband."

"What has Aymer got to do with haystacks?"

"Oh, naught. But we're not meeting in them."

"Someday you must tell me what grudge you have against haystacks." When he didn't answer, she sighed and said, "Well, I don't know where else—wait." She looked back toward the kitchen. "I have it. We'll meet in the vegetable garden. It's surrounded by high hedges, there's an arbor that will provide concealment and no one goes there at night."

"You wish to meet among the cabbages and turnips?"

"And the leeks," Honor said, wiggling her eyebrows at him.

Galen laughed. "If that dragon of a waiting woman weren't so near I'd show you what long legs are really for, my sunset."

Honor blushed and lowered her voice.

"Mayhap tonight you'll show me a little."

He shook his head. "I cannot dishonor my intended bride, even at her invitation."

"Galen de Marlowe, I did not ask you to—oooo!"

"Don't squeal like that. The pig herd will come after you."

Honor jerked her hand from his arm and lifted her chin. "As my betrothed, you should conduct yourself with courtliness and chivalry."

"Ah, but my courtliness and chivalry aren't what interest you," Galen said in a low voice. "Your gaze hardly leaves my legs unless it's to fix upon my lips. I vow I'm hard-pressed not to blush at the lascivious looks you cast my way."

"I—I do not cast—I never—" Honor stopped and turned her back on him.

"What are you doing?" he asked.

"Saying a prayer to the Blessed Virgin for patience."

She heard a clattering in the bailey and looked down to see a line of carts and wagons rolling into the castle. "I see one of my shipments from Italy has arrived at last."

She glanced back at him. He was still leering at

her, the knave. With as much dignity as she could muster, she lifted her skirts and walked toward the tower stairs.

"Pray excuse me, my lord. I must attend to this."

"Honor," he said quietly, his smile gone. "Bring the sapphire pendant tonight."

Her irritation forgotten, Honor swallowed hard at the thought of what that pendant might do to him if he touched it. "Are you certain?"

"No, but it's necessary."

She nodded. "Very well."

"And Honor."

"Yes?"

"Pray stay away from the haystacks."

She tossed a last comment over her shoulder. "Leekshanks."

He chuckled, but she hurried into the tower. She could still hear his laughter, so she raised her voice. "Leekshanks!"

IT WAS AFTER compline, and Castle Stafford was as dark as the forest of Durance Guarde except for light from the few torches along the wall walk. In her chamber, Honor pulled a black gown over her shift, picked up a velvet bag containing the sapphire pendant in one hand and grabbed her slippers in the other. The floorboards were cold as she tiptoed past the trundle bed upon which Jacoba slept. A snort made Honor jump and hold her breath. She peered into the darkness and listened. Soon she heard the steady snore that had been her sleep's accompaniment for as long as she could remember.

Outside her chamber, Honor put her slippers on and crept downstairs. In the hall she had the aid of dying torchlight by which to step over and weave her way past the servants who usually slept there. She avoided the great doors at the front of the hall and took the path that led through the screen into the buttery. She left through a small door, keeping an eye out for guards, and sped across the kitchen yard, through the herb garden, and between a gap in the hedge that separated it from the vegetable garden.

She heard the distant voices of two guards whose paths had crossed on the wall walk, and waited to make sure they weren't looking in her direction before scurrying between rows of cabbages. Close to the arbor, another man-at-arms emerged from the clock tower. Honor threw herself against the lattice that formed the walls of the arbor, hoping she'd blend in with the ivy.

The guard's sword scraped on the threshold of the clock-tower door. He paused to yawn, then turned his back and leaned over the battlements. Honor furrowed her brow as he began to fumble with his clothing. Then she sighed as it occurred to her that he was relieving himself. At the same time something grabbed her arm. Honor almost screamed, but a hand clamped over her mouth as she was pulled into the arbor.

"Mmmpf!"

"Shh. It's only me." Galen lifted his hand from her mouth. They were talking in barely audible whispers.

"I know that, curse it," Honor said. She shoved him away. "But you startled me."

"I was beginning to believe you were going to stay out there until that guard turned and saw you."

"Why is it that men believe women are naturally addlepated?"

"You ask me this at such a time? Besides, if I were the one who covered my face with white paste and posed as a ghost, I wouldn't ask such questions."

"Oh, I don't really mean you," Honor said as she searched blindly for the bench she knew sat in the arbor. Her hand hit Galen's chest. He caught it and brushed his lips against it.

Honor smiled. "I was reading one of those new translations of an ancient Greek, some fool called Aristophanes. He babbled on and on about women, how men couldn't live with them or without them."

"A wise man, Aristophanes."

"I'm going to write insulting things about men and print them with my press. We'll see how men enjoy having their whole sex scorned and abused in writing where people will read it for centuries."

Galen guided her to the bench. "Honor, did

that shipment that arrived earlier consist entirely of books?"

"Not just books," she said, growing excited. "Master Andrea del Verrocchio has a new assistant called Leonardo da Vinci, and they've sent me several paintings. We just unpacked them before I went to bed. Galen, you must see them. They have mastered perspective in painting. And the light, the images, there is nothing I can say that will prepare you for the reality of this new way of painting."

"I've heard of these men and would love to see your paintings, but we've a more urgent task to perform," Galen said.

Honor squeezed the velvet bag in her hand. "I know. I was avoiding it."

"Tell me what happened when Aymer was killed." In the darkness his hand touched her cheek. "You said you came here for a visit, and that he went out riding."

"It was over four years ago. I don't remember everything clearly."

"Try," Galen said, clasping her hand. "That part of the vision was clear. Someone hit Aymer and pushed him into the river, Honor."

"Very well." With her hand in his, her fears receded. "It was after Candlemas, I remember. The second week in February. It had snowed for a week, and that morning was the first day the sun shone. Aymer broke his fast with Father and me, but he was beset with the desire to get out of the castle after all those days spent sheltering from the snow."

Honor hesitated. "You see, Aymer had little interest in . . . That is, my company was never of much value to him." Best get it out now. She had to be honest. "I know I'm not beautiful, Galen. And Aymer was disappointed in me from the beginning. You have great patience to listen to my prattling, but Aymer was different."

There was a short silence, followed by a curse.

"Aymer had the wits of a donkey, Honor. He felt unmanned by you because he knew you were far more clever than he. That is why he avoided you."

She felt his lips brush her loose hair and her cheek.

"A man who is unmanned by a woman of intelligence is no man at all. And a man who avoids you for longer than a few minutes is a fool."

Honor turned her face to his, clasped her arms around his neck and kissed him hard. He pulled her close, only to shove away from her, breathing hard.

"Stop that, you little devil, or we'll never—your face is wet. Are you weeping?"

"N-no."

"Liar."

How could she explain? She had believed for so long that nothing so wondrous as this would ever happen to her. She had believed that her life would consist of duty and perhaps another cold alliance between her family and another. Great paintings, new knowledge from the ancient world, and fine architecture would never banish loneliness. She sniffed and wiped her eyes.

"Honor?" Galen whispered in a worried tone.

"I'm well." She slipped her hand in his again and continued. "Aymer left alone. He said he would ride until midday and return, but around noontide a storm came, full of icy rain and thunder. We grew worried, but Father said Aymer would shelter from the storm and come home when its power ebbed. When it was an hour before dark and he hadn't returned, we sent out search parties."

"Did anyone in the villages around here see him?"

"Ham the blacksmith at Holywell said Aymer stopped by shortly after noontide and bespoke a new bit and harness. Then he rode out of the town in the direction of the river Eske. That was when the storm broke. Master Baldwin's search party followed his trail along the river. Aymer must have ridden for a while, then dismounted as he neared the place where a wooden bridge crosses the Eske. He was leading his horse down the bank to the bridge when he slipped and fell in."

"He didn't slip," Galen said. "He was knocked unconscious and pushed in to drown. It's hard to recall clearly so brief a vision, but I saw a long cloak with a hood, and an arm holding a log. The cloak was lined in red and black material."

"Galen, the Stafford colors are red and black."

"I know."

They sat together, hand in hand, thinking of the significance of this new piece of the puzzle.

"I thought if anyone wanted Aymer dead it would be Isidore," Honor said at last. "He gained the title."

"I thought so, too. But it seems someone here wanted him dead for another reason."

"If you're thinking of my father—"

"I assume nothing," Galen said. "And neither should you. Did you bring the pendant?"

Reluctantly Honor produced the jewel. Holding it by the chain, she said, "You must promise to tell me all you see, and I shall take it from you if the vision seems to do you harm." She could barely see his smile.

"You imagine I may come to harm while in the midst of a vision." The smile vanished, and his lips contorted into a grimace as he looked away. "The harm comes from thinking you know what the visions mean, from cursed pride in one's gift, from thinking you can shape people's lives, when all along that power belongs to God."

"What do you mean?"

His voice grew rough. "I mean that once I sought to act upon a vision. I left my family unprotected to save another, and my enemy destroyed them."

"Dear God," Honor whispered.

She heard his anguish in the strained, thin quality of his voice. Although he'd spoken but briefly of his loss, she sensed that even this had cost him much. It was the pain in his voice that finally made her understand what torture Galen lived with every day. She remembered the attack on Argent, how Galen's wife and children had died. He still blamed himself, when the fault lay with that murderous criminal who had done the killing.

For the first time she began to understand Galen's craving for solitude. To glimpse portents, future events and past sins, and yet know that to act upon one's knowledge might bring greater evil than that one sought to prevent—it would be like living in one's own inner hell. In his position, she would have gone mad long ago.

"Honor, we haven't much time."

In the darkness she took his hand and placed the pendant in it. His hand closed; she placed hers over it and braced herself. This time Galen didn't move. Moments passed without him uttering a word. Then he sighed and opened his hand. The pendant and chain slid into Honor's grasp.

"Nothing," he said. "Whatever vision inhabited the jewel has fled."

"Good. I didn't like what happened to you when you touched it." Honor put the pendant back in the velvet pouch, relieved that he'd been spared another burdensome experience.

"Our task remains, however."

"I don't know of anyone else who might have wanted Aymer dead," she said.

"We must look at the problem differently, then," Galen said. "He was killed sometime between noontide and the hour before dusk, when Baldwin found traces of his fall into the river. Can you remember anyone who was absent from the castle during that time?"

"This is a castle, Galen. Hours can pass without my seeing someone, and yet he or she is here."

"True. Then let us try this: Who was here all the time?"

"Me, Jacoba, most of the other servants. I don't know about Sir Renard or Perkin or the men from the stables. I remember the cook because he asked me what I would like prepared for the following day." Honor thought for a few moments. "It's no use. I can't remember anyone else. Isidore was the one who gained the most from Aymer's death. He could have stalked him secretly, killed him, and ridden away without coming near Castle Stafford."

"You may be correct," Galen said. "But try to remember more details about that day. Was there something to mark it as different from any other day?"

Honor grabbed Galen's arm. "I don't recall, but I know how we might discover it. We'll look in Master Baldwin's household accounts." This was much better than vision. Accounts were tangible, real, and they posed no risk to Galen.

"Won't he be curious about why you wish to see them?"

"If he asks, I'll tell him I want to model my own after his. Besides, the old ones are kept in the storeroom next to the treasury. We can look at them when he's busy elsewhere. He won't even know we've read them."

"Excellent. It's a beginning."

"You're certain about the colors," Honor said. "Red and black."

"Aye, my little sunset. I'm certain."

She heard him sigh.

"Honor, I must speak of—"

Her fingers found his lips and pressed them closed. "No more. If you suspect my father, you're wrong."

"No, I'm not talking about that."

"Then it can wait, can it not?" Honor shivered. "The night grows chilly though the day was warm."

Galen stood, threw his cloak around her, and pulled her into his arms. Honor snuggled against his body and turned her face so that she could nuzzle his neck.

"Honor, don't. You don't understand."

She nibbled the soft skin near his throat, and Galen nearly cried out. His body stiffened, and in seconds Honor was on her back on the bench.

"God's mercy, Honor, I wish you hadn't done that."

"Why?" She heard him swear.

"Lady Honor Jennings," he said as he held her

beneath him, "I suppose you've noticed that I desire you."

Honor was distracted by the feel of his legs against hers. "Um, yes."

"Yes," he echoed, "but what escapes you is that you've possessed me more thoroughly than the most powerful of my visions. Awake or asleep, hungry or starving, idle or occupied, rested or exhausted, it doesn't matter. You're there, in my thoughts."

"I know what men—"

He silenced her by placing his lips near her ear and saying, "It's not mere lust. It's much more. I can't escape it, and I've tried. I've tried to make sense of it, and I finally discovered the answer."

Honor didn't want him to stop talking, because his breath in her ear sent exquisite jolts of pleasure through her body. "What is the answer?"

"I'm possessed because you're always tripping or stumbling and falling down, you see. You end up in the most enticing positions. I never met a woman who spends so much time spread out on the ground. And of course I fear for you each time you go crashing down, which increases the excitement."

Honor almost lost track of what he was saying because he nuzzled her cheek.

"So you see, my little sunset, you're the one who has worked the sorcery, not me." He arched his back and gasped. "Not me."

She had only a moment to wonder at the pain

in his voice. Galen's mouth discovered hers even as she discovered the delights she'd coveted beneath his hose. As her hands massaged their way down his legs and up again, she heard her gown tear and felt his hand on her breast. Long moments passed during which they explored each other's mouth. Then his lips touched her breast.

Fire exploded inside her. This was unlike any touch she'd ever experienced—gentle yet insistent, urging, burning. Nearly mad with the deluge of sensations from his hands and mouth, Honor began to move, pressing up against him while pulling him against her at the same time. She heard him try to say something, but her hand found him, and he cried out. He responded with touches so intimate, yet light and unceasing, that she dug her nails into his back and rose up from the bench.

"God forgive me," he groaned.

She felt him press against her, felt him inside her. All reason fled as pleasure invaded, climbed, and burst over her. Galen stifled her cries with his mouth, then did the same with his own. They subsided, him resting on her heavily for a moment before moving to relieve her of his weight. Still gasping, Honor smiled into the darkness at the joy of her discovery. Galen rested his head on her breast. She ran her fingers through his soft hair, but he lifted his head suddenly.

"Oh, damnation and sin."

"A sin readily put right when we marry." Honor took his hand and kissed it. "And one for which

SIXTEEN

THE DAY AFTER he made love to Honor, Galen woke with an overwhelming urge to flee Castle Stafford. In a few short weeks he'd managed to ruin his life. He'd conducted himself with so little governance and honor that he was now doomed to marry Honor Jennings when he'd never had such an intention.

To make his sin worse, he'd taken her love without being honest about the circumstances of their betrothal. And worst of all, he still didn't understand his feelings. The only things of which he was certain were that he wanted Honor desperately, that he didn't want to hurt her, and that he most certainly would.

Determined to at least reduce that certainty, he sought her out in her solar with the intention of confessing all. She hardly listened to his greeting, however, quickly dragging him to look at Master Baldwin's old accounts.

"I was just coming to find you," she said. "Everyone's busy right now. Your brothers went with Father to call on the sheriff. They're old drinking companions, you know. And everyone else is occupied with the hay harvest."

"First I—"

She grabbed his hand and pulled him along. "We must go now. Jacoba is going to keep watch."

He glanced back to find his nemesis stalking along in his wake, her bushy brows meeting in the middle of her forehead, her thick fists bunched.

"Honor, you promised not to tell anyone."

"I didn't tell her much. Just that I'm investigating an important injustice, and you're helping me." She tugged his hand. "Now come quickly."

He allowed her to lead him out of the hall, across the ward to the thickest, highest tower of the castle. It had once been a keep, but had been remodeled and put to use as a treasury, storehouse, and records office. Honor nodded to the sentry beside the door in the base of the tower.

"This, my lord, is the treasury," she said for the benefit of the guard. "Not as large as yours at Argent, I vow, but a goodly fortress all the same."

Galen kept his face impassive. "Indeed, a most, er, fortified fortress."

Behind him Jacoba sniggered. Honor opened the door with one of the keys suspended from her girdle. Beckoning him inside, she put her hand on his arm and continued her description of the treasury.

"Of course, the room with the bars and the giant lock is the main treasury. There you see the chamber where the most valuable spices are kept, and that one houses the costly fabrics and such."

When Jacoba shut the door on the guard, Honor grinned at Galen. "The record chamber is upstairs."

Clasping his hand like an excited child, Honor pulled him upstairs and into a room filled with accounts that had been bound into books and stacked one on top of the other. A table sat in the middle of the room, and it too was covered. Stacks of loose papers, bills of lading, receipts, and registers of laborers from the past year lay waiting for someone to put them in order. An old, blunt quill lay on top of a stack of used parchment. Nearby a bottle of ink had dried almost to powder. Honor opened the single window that looked out on the inner ward and lit several candles.

"Jacoba, go back downstairs and watch. Run up here if anyone comes in."

"Yes, me lady."

Jacoba gave him a warning scowl and left. Galen opened his mouth, determined to get the truth out, but Honor spoke.

"Don't just stand there." She plopped a dusty bound volume into his hands. "We haven't much time. Master Baldwin may return from his survey of the haying anytime now. If he has to make a payment to a bailiff or reeve, he could be here within moments."

She shoved papers aside on the table and indicated that he should put the heavy volume down. He complied and opened it.

Honor turned the pages swiftly, then pointed. "You see. Here it is. February."

His good intentions would have to wait, it seemed. He read lists of payments for spices, salt, wax, candles. Honor pointed out disbursements of alms by Theodoric.

"Quite a large sum," he said.

"Theodoric is most conscientious and can't refuse someone in need."

Galen perused page after page of expenses for meals, who was present and for how long. Baldwin was meticulous, even noting what was left after a meal and that two friars from Norwich stopped at the castle and what they consumed before continuing on their journey to London. It went on, day after day, month after month. He turned back to the pages dealing with February.

"I see your father's favorite falcon received a special diet."

Honor nodded. "He was sick."

"More lists of what was consumed: loaves of bread, joints, porridge, wine, herring, oysters, mutton. Hay for the horses. What's this?" He picked up a scrap of parchment that had been inserted into the book.

Honor looked over his shoulder. A long lock of copper hair swung against his cheek, and Galen rubbed it against his skin, almost forgetting the task at hand.

"Oh, I remember. That was when Father had Baldwin add the new brewhouse beside the kitchen. There's an especially thick wall between the two so that if the kitchen does catch fire, the brewhouse is better protected. Of course, with a stone kitchen, the chance of fire is much less."

Galen moved the scrap of parchment aside and was about to turn the page, then stopped. "Honor, look."

There among the list of people fed at the castle table on the day after Aymer was killed was Isidore Jennings.

"Yes," Honor said. "Once Aymer vanished, he came. It's only natural."

"But look. He's listed among those at breakfast as well as dinner and supper."

They looked at each other. Galen said, "He must have been on his way to Castle Stafford before Aymer died."

Honor's eyes grew round, and she nodded slowly. "So he was in the vicinity?"

"Aye, my love. It seems you may have been right to suspect Isidore. What? Why do you gawk at me like that?"

"Say it again."

"You may have been right."

"No. Say, 'my love' again. I can't seem to believe you're really saying it, no matter how many times I hear it."

To his surprise, Galen felt himself flush. He lowered his eyes.

"By my faith, you're blushing!"

He heard Honor giggle, and set his jaw.

"Who would have believed it?" she said in a wondering tone. "My gallant, mysterious, and dangerous Lord Galen de Marlowe is shy."

"No, Honor, it's not that."

A raucous din suddenly began in the ward and reached them through the window. Hearing his name bellowed, Galen set his jaw, went to the window and found his brothers, horses in tow, standing in the ward. He stuck his head out the window.

"Cease your caterwauling. What do you want?"

Fabron put his hands on his hips and affected surprise. "Oh, are you up there, brother? We've been looking for you. You promised to show us Durance Guarde today."

"Go away. I'm not ready yet."

Simon walked over to stand beneath the window and gave him a look of such suppressed rage that Galen was taken aback. "Not feeling well today, dear brother? *Eat too many vegetables last night?*"

Galen felt as if he would explode with wrath. He searched the ward and snarled, "Where's Fulk?"

"He's not feeling well either," Simon growled. "Won't come out of his chamber."

Pointing at Simon, Galen said, "You stay right there. I'll show you Durance Guarde. By God's teeth, I will."

He whirled around to find Honor staring at him with frightened indigo eyes.

"What's wrong?"

"Naught that should concern you, my little sunset." Galen managed a stiff smile. "I fear my brothers have a nasty habit of interfering in my personal life, and it's time to make them stop. Such a task may prove difficult and . . . shall I say, rough—but it must be done. It's better managed away from here. I'll talk to them at Durance Guarde, which is far enough away that our shouting won't disturb you."

He left the storeroom with Honor trailing behind him.

"Now, Galen," she said. "Don't be too harsh. Your brothers worship you. They have since they were children, and they worry about you."

"The time for worry is long past. I'm quite capable of leading my own life." Galen stopped as they reached the door where Jacoba stood guard and took Honor by the shoulders. "I have to make them understand this, Honor. Do you want them interfering between us after we're married?"

"Oh, no." She smiled and kissed his cheek. "Do what you must, and I'll finish here."

"Don't stay long," he said. "Remember, we don't want to attract attention with our inquiries. And don't do anything else until I return."

"Don't worry about me," she said, taking his hand and bringing it up to her cheek.

The touch of her skin brought last night back as if it were happening all over again. Galen sucked in air and squeezed her hand. Her eyes were burning into his. He took her hands and kissed them.

"By the Trinity, what have you done to me?"

He turned and left before he made a fool of himself. Each step away from her was difficult, but he knew better than to allow his brothers to corner him with Honor present. There was going to be an affray, a nasty little battle of wills, and he was going to win it. He jerked the reins of his horse from Simon's grasp, mounted and burst into motion, cantering over the drawbridge. In moments he'd left his brothers scrambling to catch up with him.

The chase continued until he reached Durance Guarde. By the time he walked his horse over the rickety bridge and under the vine-covered arches of the ruin, his anger had turned cold and vitriolic. He dismounted before the old keep and waited until his brothers straggled into the castle ward.

When they'd all dismounted, breathless and sweating, he walked over to Simon and said lightly, "Now, sweet Simon, before you say anything, allow me to tell you that should any of you thrust yourselves between me and Lady Honor again in such a manner, I will issue a challenge and see to it that none of you leaves the field except on a stretcher."

"You're mistaken, Galen," Simon replied, un-fazed by the threat. "We care nothing for what you do with—for your attentions to Lady Honor. That's your own affair, but you're rooting around for Aymer Jennings' murderer without us," Simon said.

"I can't have you great louts blundering around. This is a matter of delicacy."

"It's dangerous," Fabron said. "Five are stronger than one."

"If I need you, I shall call upon you."

Macaire shook his head. "Simon, you never suc-ceeded in forcing Galen to do anything he didn't want to do. You shouldn't have used Fulk."

Galen eyed Simon, who looked away.

"You made him use his gift to find out about me."

"I was worried."

Fabron shrugged. "Admit it, Simon. You're afraid for Galen and don't want to say so."

"Well." Simon dug the heel of his boot into the dirt. He darted a quick look at Galen. "Did you tell her yet?"

Galen pressed his lips together, unwilling to let go of his anger, but Simon's face bore such anxiety for him that he had to relent.

"No, you great lummox. She's too caught up with finding out what happened to Aymer. And too busy planning." His voice lowered so that they could barely hear him. "Too happy. She chatters a lot when she's happy."

SEVENTEEN

HONOR WATCHED GALEN and his brothers leave and stood contemplating the busy ward from the treasury tower window. The falconer walked from the dovecote to the mews. She could hear clanging from the smithy. Across from the stables Sir Renard was teaching Dagobert a few elementary moves in swordplay. The boy swiped at the knight with his wooden sword with more vigor than precision.

She smiled at the boy. She smiled all the time now, which irritated Jacoba. Honor wished she could share her secret, but the waiting woman would be upset that her vigilance on Honor's behalf had failed.

This morning in the chapel she had withdrawn from the order of vowesses, and tomorrow morning she would sign more official papers having to do with property and wealth. Galen had brought several chests with him, the contents of which he refused to reveal until tomorrow, and Honor's curiosity was aroused. But he couldn't give her a gift more precious than himself, and that he'd already done.

What was she doing staring out the window like a half-wit? Honor returned to the table to peruse the castle records once more, but all she saw were mundane lists of supplies. Every servant and dependent at the castle got a new gown each year, so there was plenty of red and black fabric in store. Master Baldwin saw to it that no roof leaked, that the cistern was always in good repair, and that the fireplaces in the kitchen and brewhouse were in good order. The year Aymer died had been an especially busy time for repairs and refurbishing.

Someone was stomping up the stairs. It was Jacoba deliberately making a great noise. Honor closed the account book and shoved it among several on a shelf. She flew to the window and was standing there gazing out at the haystacks when Jacoba hurried in, out of breath.

"Me lady, Master Baldwin and others follow me directly."

Honor nodded, shooed Jacoba farther inside, and raised her voice. "You see, Jacoba, the view from this window is quite good. I think Father would refurbish this tower for my lord and myself."

Baldwin appeared in the doorway with Theodoric and Perkin behind him. "My lady?"

"Ah, greetings, Master Baldwin." Honor sailed over to him and nodded at the others. "I was just thinking that the treasury tower would make excellent quarters once I'm married."

"Oh, my lady," said Baldwin, "this old place isn't worthy. Besides, to make it comfortable, we would have to put in new chimneys."

"But you're so good at remodeling," Honor said. "I remember how you put in that fireplace in the brewery, and it works excellent well." Honor turned and walked around the chamber, pretending to glance for the first time at the records on the shelves. "That was the same year my husband had his accident. A terrible time. May God rest his soul."

Baldwin gave her a confused look, and then all emotion seemed to leave his face. Honor glanced at the other two, who wore the impassive looks of servants who didn't wish to reveal their low opinion of a nobleman. It was a peculiar expression that reminded Honor of a constipated cow. Aymer had seldom thought about any of these men, not because he disliked them, but because he viewed servants as he did furniture or livestock.

Once Theodoric had begged Aymer to intercede on behalf of a poor peasant who had lost his crop and animals. Aymer had refused and the family had died during the harsh winter. Perkin simply hated

Aymer because, when hunting, Aymer rode over crops, through orchards and trampled gardens in pursuit of game. To Perkin, his plants and trees were his children. His sister's family lived on Jennings' land and had been the victims of Aymer's ruthless riding habits. Honor knew that Aymer had been oblivious to the hatred he provoked. And had he known, he wouldn't have cared.

Honor looked into Baldwin's concerned eyes. This man had been steward here since before she was born. His opinion would count for much.

"Baldwin, I would like you to think back to that time, the day my husband died. Was there anything amiss? Anything out of the ordinary?"

"It had been snowing hard for a long time, my lady. Is there anything wrong? You seem to be troubled."

She sighed and decided she'd gone as far as she could. Galen wouldn't want her to stir up suspicions among the castle folk.

"No. I suppose my betrothal has brought back memories of that unhappy time. I do wish we had been able to recover Lord Jennings' body. He had no proper burial, and . . ." Her voice faded. "Ah, well."

"A most tragic circumstance, my lady. And now, if you've no need of me, I have alms to disburse for Theodoric, and Perkin must pay the undergardeners."

"Of course, you may go."

Baldwin bowed and left, followed by the other two men. Jacoba trailed after them, having a chat with Perkin about apples for cider. Honor could hear the great iron key turn in the treasury lock, and the barred gate swing open. She wandered back to the table, where she picked up the scrap of parchment that had been left out of the account book she'd replaced on its shelf. Her finger traced an item, payment for bricks used in the brewhouse wall and fireplace. Her finger moved on, then strayed back and stayed on the bricks.

"Bricks," she murmured. "Poor Baldwin deals with such tedious work."

It was a good thing she'd rescued Dagobert from following in his grandfather's footsteps. The boy would have hated dealing with numbers and petty details of shillings and pence. Perkin was lucky that Aymer had died before Castle Stafford came to him, or the gardens would have been reduced by half.

Honor picked up the parchment and searched the shelves for the account book to which it belonged. She walked along, then stopped. She tapped the parchment against the bookbindings. Then the tapping stopped.

"By my faith," she said aloud. She tapped her forefinger against her temple and squeezed her eyes shut. "What did Galen say? What did he say? He said: hay—no, hoes—tack and bricks. What else?" She pounded her fist in her palm. "Beshrew my pitiful memory. He said hoes, tack, bricks... spices! Yes, spices and falcons and ale. That was it. What have all these in common?" She went silent as she followed a path of reasoning.

"Oh, no." Her hand crumpled the parchment. "No. It can't be."

Picking up her skirts, Honor hurried out of the storeroom. Downstairs she passed Jacoba and Perkin.

"Jacoba, I'm going riding."

"I'll come immediately."

"There's no need," Honor said as she left the tower. "I've something urgent I wish to tell Lord Galen. I'll join him and his brothers, and they're certainly more than enough of an escort."

For once Jacoba didn't argue. "Aye, me lady. With all them young brutes, I've no fear for your safety."

It didn't take long for Honor to ride to Durance Guarde. She hadn't bothered to change clothes, and soon she was dismounting and tethering her horse alongside Galen's in the makeshift stable. She hadn't seen the de Marlowe brothers on her way in, or in the bailey. They had to be inside the keep, because Galen's servant Ralph was sitting on the wooden stairs before the tower. He had been munching on a meat pie when Honor rode up, and was busy stuffing the last of it in his mouth when she mounted the stairs. He packed pastry into his mouth and scrambled to his feet before the door.

"Gree-ings, m'la-y."

She inclined her head. "Good day to you, Ralph. I see you enjoy cook's mutton as much as the rest of us."

"In-dee, m'la-y. Lor-ship's in—" Ralph coughed, spluttering flakes of crust. "Lordship's inside."

"Good." She tried to walk around him, but Ralph moved into her way.

"I'll fetch 'is lordship for you, m'lady."

"No need." She tried to go past him again, but he moved again.

"It would be better so, m'lady."

"Why? What are you hiding? What's he doing that I cannot see?"

"Oh, it ain't nothing like that, m'lady. It's just that 'is lordship don't like to be surprised."

"I am hardly a surprise, and I've urgent news for him." She tried yet again to go past the servant, and again he stepped in her way. Honor narrowed her eyes, pulled herself up to her full height, and said carefully, "Ralph, if you want that mutton pie to stay in your stomach, you'd better get out of my way."

"But m'lady, 'is lordship won't like it."

Honor pointed down the stairs with a stiff arm. "Go. At once."

"But—"

She made a fist and raised it, knowing Ralph's stomach was bursting with food. Ralph shied away from her and went down the stairs slowly, casting anxious looks at her all the way. She made shooing motions.

"Run along. Water my horse."

"Aye, m'lady." Ralph vanished into the stables.

Curious as to what made the servant so reluctant to allow her inside, Honor opened the door slowly and peeked inside. The hall was deserted, so she climbed the winding stairs. She searched the gallery and several towers. Finally, in Berengar's Tower, she noticed that the ladder to the roof was bathed in sunlight.

She went to it and heard voices. The de Marlowe men were on the roof. They must have been looking elsewhere, or they would have seen her ride into the bailey. Or else they were too engrossed in their conversation to pay attention to anything else.

Putting her foot on the first rung of the ladder, Honor climbed up, taking care not to catch her foot in her hem. She almost fell when she dropped her skirt and stepped on it. Backing down one rung, she gathered more fabric in one hand and began to climb again. The last thing she wanted was to hurt herself before the betrothal ceremony. Relatives would begin to arrive soon for the wedding, and she'd hate to greet them with a limp. Galen would scold her, but not for long when she gave him her news.

She had almost reached the open trapdoor. Sunlight bathed her face as she heard Galen speak in a voice so tortured she froze where she was.

"None of you has had to face this choice, damn you. Simon, you married a distant cousin who already knew. You other two have yet to settle upon a mate, and God help the woman who takes you."

Honor heard Simon reply in an impatient tone. "Jesu protect me from such a nice conscience as yours, brother. So you were forced to offer for her because she discovered your visions. People marry for less honorable reasons all the time. Besides, you like her. She's pleasant, if a bit daft and frazzle-headed from trying to do fifty things at once. You've done the most important thing. You've made her love you. She'll never betray our secret, for fear of losing you."

"Chivalry and honor demand that I tell her the truth, by God! I'll not begin on a lie."

Honor stopped listening because her body seemed to have grown so cold she might as well have been lying beneath a frozen lake. Then humiliation flooded her, melting her frozen body and leaving her weak. Her hands shook, her stomach churned, and she gagged. She leaned against the ladder for a moment, gulping in air. Then, slowly, with a force of will she hadn't suspected, she climbed up the last three steps of the ladder and onto the roof, her original purpose forgotten.

Galen and his brothers were standing at the battlements looking over the forest treetops. As she stepped away from the trapdoor, Galen must have seen movement out of the corner of his eye, for he turned quickly.

"Honor," he said.

She winced at the fear she heard in his voice, then smoothed her features into a mask of indifference. "It seems I've come upon most secret talking, my lords."

Galen walked swiftly over to her, but she held up a hand in warning, and he stopped halfway there.

Honor possessed a tone of voice she seldom used. She used it on negligent and unredeemable servants, on dishonest tradesmen and the like. She heard herself use it now, and marveled at its effect.

"I straightly charge and command you, Lord Galen, to keep yourself from me."

"Honor, please."

"I am grievously offended by your dishonesty and trickery," she said quietly. She hid her shaking hands in the folds of her skirts.

"I'm so sorry, Honor, but if you'll but listen, I can make all clear."

She hardly looked at Galen. Glancing around at his brothers, who seemed to have become stuck in place, she said, "I pray you, don't trouble yourself. We will end this betrothal as soon as the clerks and lawyers can arrange it."

She put a trembling hand on the ladder and gave Galen a frozen look. "Such a drastic measure was hardly necessary to ensure my silence on your behalf. It is not necessary now. Your secret will go with me to the tomb, but I need not burden myself with a reluctant husband on the way there."

Galen moved then, putting his hand on hers where it clasped the ladder. Honor gasped and jerked her hand out of reach.

"No!" She calmed herself and went on, lips and voice quivering. "If you do indeed value chivalry, you will refrain from touching one to whom your very presence is like hell upon this earth."

Honor got herself down the ladder as quickly as she could. It was a miracle she didn't fall down it. Galen looked down at her, preparing to follow.

"You needn't concern yourself, my lord. I intend to ride directly back to Castle Stafford and inform my father of our break. We will do this according to my wishes, as the beginning of this betrothal was according to yours. We'll postpone the betrothal ceremony, wait a decent interval, and then I shall declare that I no longer care for the alliance. I shall choose a worthy replacement for you. It shouldn't be too difficult to find a better match than you. But remember, it is I who shall rebuff you." She leaned forward to look into his eyes. "And you, my lord, will behave with decent humility and sorrow. After a few months, you may resume your old life."

"My love—"

"Say that again and I'll come up there and cut out your tongue."

"Honor, I pray you to forgive me. I didn't mean for this to happen. What can I do?"

"I care not what you do. Stay in this place, if

you like. Stay at Durance Guarde for the rest of your life. I shall not come here again."

Turning on her heel, Honor walked to the stairs and descended. She was lucky her knees didn't buckle before she reached the hall. She didn't hear anything or see much as she went to the stables. She didn't remember how she got on her mare. But she woke from her daze when Galen came charging out of the keep yelling her name. Her mare reared, and Honor lunged forward to keep her seat. Steadying her horse, she gave her former betrothed a cold glance. As he ran toward her, she kicked the mare, and the horse sprang across the ward.

She was out of Durance Guarde before she heard Galen bellow. When she'd reached the stables, thanks be to God she'd had the presence of mind to order Ralph to loose the other horses. She would be well away before Galen caught one and saddled it. But she wouldn't go home. Not yet. She needed time to face what had happened. Time to steel herself to confront her father.

Choosing a direction at random, Honor urged the mare forward deeper into the forest of Durance Guarde. Soon she'd lose the afternoon sun in the thick canopy, but it didn't matter. The sun had set in her world anyway.

"Stupid. Stupid, stupid, witless fool. To think a man like that would want you."

She allowed the mare to walk unhindered, for tears blinded her to the path ahead. Great sobs wracked her body. The mare kept walking, and Honor bent over the horse's neck, moaning in pain. She'd lost Galen—her beloved, enticing, incomparable Galen.

No, she hadn't lost him; she had never had him at all.

EIGHTEEN

GALEN KICKED HIS horse, forcing him to crash through tangled undergrowth and overhanging vines. Breathing harshly, he cursed as he had countless times since Honor had vanished into the forest of Durance Guarde. Far away he heard Simon calling Honor's name, and knew that his brothers had had no more luck than he in finding her. She had ridden into the depths of the woods and vanished. She was good at it.

His heart beat so fast Galen was certain it would break his ribs. He'd been searching for over two hours. Hacking at brambles and vines with his sword he burst through the undergrowth into a clearing where the stream cut through an outcrop of rocks. He pulled his horse to a stop. His eyes darted methodically around the space, looking for hoofprints, broken branches, anything that would mark her passage. He found none.

"Damnation and sin!"

The violence of his words caused his horse to dance. He calmed the animal, then rested his forearms on the pommel of his saddle and lowered his head. Pain roiled deep within his body, a pain of the spirit that manifested itself in physical torment.

Now he knew what a ghost really looked like. He'd seen one when Honor appeared on the roof of Berengar's Tower. Her face had the pallor of a shade. Not the false, slick white she'd put on it to play Rowena's ghost, but the ashen shade of brilliant, transparent skin drained of life. He had caused that transformation. He, with his blind, ass-witted stupidity.

In the instant he saw her, he'd known without a doubt that he had lost her. In that moment he understood himself as he had not since meeting this entrancing bundle of liveliness and wit. Now that it might be too late, he knew he'd loved her almost from the beginning. There had been no choice, no reflection, no steady growth of affection. One moment he was alone, and the next she was in his life, inside his mind and body, provoking him, teasing him, never to depart. If he hadn't been so determined to protect himself from being hurt again, he would have understood this. How ironic that in sealing off his heart like a tomb entrance, he'd caused himself the pain he'd been trying to avoid.

Galen dismounted and led his horse to the stream. While the animal drank, he splashed water on his face and neck. Sitting on a rock, he put two fingers in his mouth and whistled loudly. His brothers would come to him upon hearing this signal. He remained on that rock, descending further into a black fugue until Simon rode into the clearing. His brother dismounted and watered his horse without speaking. Macaire soon arrived, followed by Fabron. None of them spoke while the horses drank.

Finally Galen rose and gathered the reins of his mount. "I'm returning to Castle Stafford."

"Galen." Simon walked over to stand beside his older brother. "I'm sorry."

Galen didn't answer. He didn't trust himself.

"He's not angry with us," Fabron said.

Macaire collapsed on the rock where Galen had been sitting. "He's mad at himself for being such an arse."

"For not realizing how besotted he was," Fabron finished.

All three of them looked at him. Galen returned their gazes, one at a time. Each looked away.

"If any of you dares interfere again, I'll put the lot of you in the dungeon at Durance Guarde until you learn to mind your own affairs."

"Now, Galen," Fabron said.

Galen wasn't listening. He mounted his horse and headed out of the clearing. "Search until dusk, then return. I'm going back to the castle to see if she's there."

Although he pushed his horse to the limit, the journey back to the castle took more time than Galen wished, but once he was dismounted before the hall at Castle Stafford he realized something. He must be discreet in searching for Honor, or he'd alarm Sir Walter, Jacoba—the whole castle, in fact. He handed his reins to Wilfred the groom and asked if Lady Honor had returned.

"No, my lord. At least, her mare isn't in the stables yet."

Galen nodded and was running up the steps to the hall when Fulk came out to meet him.

"Have you seen Honor?" Galen asked without a greeting.

Fulk shook his head. "I'm sorry. It all went wrong, didn't it?"

"Yes, thanks to my willful blindness."

"Ah, you know now. I hope it's not too late."

Galen touched Fulk's sleeve. "Is it?"

Fulk gave him a sad smile. "You give me too much credit. I don't know the lady well enough. As for where she might be, even I can't tell you that. It is beyond my power."

"Very well," Galen said. "Then will you see to it that Sir Walter is occupied and doesn't become alarmed at Honor's absence? She heard us talking about why I made the offer of marriage, and now she thinks I care nothing for her. She ran, and I can't find her. Her mare isn't in the stables, but she might have instructed someone to walk the horse to cool it down. I want to speak to her before she tells her father she won't marry me."

"I'll do what I can," Fulk said.

Muttering his thanks, Galen went into the hall. A glance told him Honor wasn't there. Servants were setting tables in preparation for supper, so he pretended to wander past the screen, through the service areas and out to the kitchen. Having no success, he quickly surveyed the inner ward as he returned to the hall. Mayhap Honor had simply gone to her chamber. He ran upstairs and came face-to-face with Jacoba outside Honor's room. The waiting woman frowned at him.

Approaching her with caution, Galen asked, "Has your mistress returned?"

"No, me lord. Thought she was with you. Here, what do you mean where is she? You don't know? Have you lost her?"

"No, no, no." Galen backed away. "We seemed to have—um—missed each other."

Jacoba's ruddy face settled into a bull-like expression. "Begging your pardon, me lord, but I don't see as how that could happen. She knew right where you was going." She followed him to the stair landing as he backed away, her head cocked to the side. "What've you done with her?"

"Naught. I've done nothing. I'll find her. Pray go about your business, my good woman."

He was unprepared when Jacoba pounced on him. She pushed him against the banister and thrust her face close to his.

"She rode out special to tell you something important, she did. And now you come skulking back without her. What did you do? If you've hurt her, I'll give you such a beating, lord or no."

Jacoba raised her fist and leaned over him. Galen bent back over the banister, glancing at the long drop to the hall below. His eyes widened, and he dodged aside, retreating down several steps. Jacoba came after him.

"All right!" He raised his hands in surrender. "We had a misunderstanding. It was my fault, and I wish to prostrate myself at her feet. Does that satisfy you?"

"No," Jacoba snapped. "Where is she?"

"I don't know. She ran away."

Jacoba stopped on the third step and folded her substantial arms across her even more substantial chest. "Then she don't want to be found, and I ain't helping you."

"Look out the window, woman. Dusk approaches, and neither my brothers nor I have been able to find her. She was terribly distressed when she left Durance Guarde. Something could have happened to her."

The hard look left Jacoba's face. " 'Ow long's she been gone?"

Galen ran a hand through his hair. "I don't know. It seems like hours and hours." He slumped down on a step and put his face in his hands. "I'm such a miserable arse."

"Humph. I ain't disagreeing."

Galen didn't bother replying. He was staring at his boots, trying to think, when Jacoba surprised him by sitting down next to him.

"You look as sick as a ewe with a breeched lamb." She studied him some more, then said, "Reckon you're not going away, are you?"

"Never."

"If you've hurt her, she'll shut herself up and go all cold inside. Mighty hard to get to her through that mountain o' ice."

"I don't care how hard it is."

Jacoba examined his face for a long while, then whacked him on the back.

"Ouch!"

"You might just be worthy of her after all."

"I doubt that."

"Me too, but she wants you, so I got no choice. I'll just have to see to it that you don't disappoint her no more. Her first husband was an arse, you know." Jacoba looked at him sideways. "Speaking of arses, Lord Aymer spent a lot o' time inna guarderobe lots of times being sick after he done something mean to her. Had some painful bouts regarding his digestion, did Lord Aymer."

"I shall remember that," Galen said. "Now, Mistress Jacoba, will you help me?"

Jacoba scratched beneath her headscarf. "When

she left Lady Honor said she had something particular urgent to tell you."

"What?"

"Don't know. She talked to Perkin, Theodoric,
and Master Baldwin in the record storeroom for a
bit. Then she came downstairs, and I could see she
was excited. She left right quick."

Galen thought quickly, and as he did, his anxiety turned to dread. Honor must have discovered
something important about Aymer's murder after
he left her. What if she'd betrayed herself to the
guilty one? God's mercy, there might be more to
her disappearance than just that abysmal confrontation at Durance Guarde.

Fighting back panic, Galen looked at Jacoba. "If
Honor is upset, where does she go?"

"If me lady is really upset, she prays in the
chapel."

Galen rose and hurried downstairs with Jacoba
trundling after him. They almost ran across the
ward. The sun was beginning to sink below
the battlements as they entered the chapel,
where Theodoric and the Stafford chaplain were
preparing for vespers. The two clergymen turned
around as Galen and Jacoba rushed in. They skittered to a halt at the disapproving looks they received. Kneeling, they crossed themselves, and
got up again.

Galen hissed at Jacoba, "She's not here."

The waiting woman grasped his sleeve and

tugged him outside. "This ain't like her. If she was terrible hurt, she'd be in there."

They stood outside the chapel beneath its stained-glass windows, each at a loss. Galen leaned against the stone wall below the window and glared at the piggery, his anxiety growing with each passing moment. Then he gave the falcon mews a scowl. Suddenly he charged toward the stables. Jacoba ran after him.

"Where are you going, me lord?"

"Mayhap she's returned and we missed her."

He rushed inside to find Wilfred putting hay in the mangers while another groom filled water troughs. The stall that sheltered Honor's mare was empty. His heart pounding, Galen headed outside.

"By my faith, I hate this," he muttered. "She's upset enough and stubborn enough to remain out all night." He ran a hand through his hair, forgetting he wasn't alone. "There's no telling what's happened to her."

Luckily the waiting woman mistook his meaning. "Afraid you're right, me lord. She was that determined to get you out of Durance Guarde. Traipsed all through that demon-infested forest at night, dragging us with her."

Galen almost smiled as he thought of Honor haunting the ruins in her ragged white gown. He stopped suddenly and looked at Jacoba. "Durance Guarde."

"Aye, me lord?"

"She's a clever little devil. She knew we'd be

looking for her everywhere but the place she ran from."

Jacoba grinned at him. "I vow you're right, me lord."

Galen whirled around and hurried to the stables again. He had to find Honor. He was certain she'd blundered into danger. He could almost feel it like a vision. A vision. An image of Honor and a tower threatened to drown him in images of death. He fought off the vision with a desperation that gave him a strength he'd never had before. There was no time for visions or dithering over what to do. He glanced at Jacoba as they entered the stables.

"When my brothers return, tell them where I've gone."

"I will, me lord. You just bring her back safe."

"Fear not, Jacoba. I'm not coming back without her."

He took a fresh horse and, riding recklessly, covered the distance to Durance Guarde in half the time it usually took. Still, when he rode into the bailey it was dark. He didn't see Honor's mare, but she might have hidden the animal as a precaution against his return. Where would she go to lick her wounds? Not Berengar's Tower, where he had been, but the image of a tower kept thrusting itself into his mind. But which one? Which would Honor chose?

"Rowena's Tower, by my faith."

Galen ran into the dark keep, but was forced to search for a torch to light his way. He found one and ran through the vast ruin as fast as he could without causing the light to go out, a feeling of urgent danger driving him on. He reached Rowena's Tower and burst into the lady's chamber only to find it deserted. His heart felt like it dropped to his boots. His shoulders slumped, and he walked over to the window at which Honor had posed as Rowena's ghost. Thrusting the torch into a sconce, he propped a shoulder against the window and stared across the empty space that separated this tower from Berengar's.

Just as he was contemplating the possibility that he could lose Honor forever, the moon rose over Berengar's Tower. Wisps of clouds sailed across the brilliant orb as it crested the battlements. Galen shoved himself erect as the clouds drifted past and the moon shone brighter, revealing a figure in silhouette against the white disk.

He knew that curved figure; it was etched inside his mind more indelibly than the carving on his sword hilt. He opened his mouth, but before he could call out, Honor moved. She was moving backward. Then he saw the second figure, taller, male. Suddenly it rushed at her. Galen shouted, but his cry was drowned by Honor's. He raced out of Rowena's chamber and hurtled into Berengar's Tower. Taking the steps three at once, he was breathless by the time he climbed the ladder to the roof. He burst outside, into a stiff breeze, his gaze darting around the circular space. The man had backed Honor against the battlements, and Galen rushed at them as he heard her strangled cries.

His pounding footsteps must have warned the attacker, for he turned at the last moment. Too late Galen saw the club in his hand. He tried to dodge the blow, but the weapon caught him on the side of his head. The impact stunned him, and when he could see again, the attacker was standing over him, the club raised for a deathblow.

Galen gasped and rolled as the club struck. As he moved he heard a small roar, then a shriek from the attacker. He got up and saw Honor clinging to the man's back. She'd wrapped her legs around his waist and was tearing at his hair, trying to scratch his eyes.

Galen stumbled toward them, drawing his sword, when Honor bit the man's ear. The man bellowed, dropped the club and thrashed about, trying to get a grip on her head. He threw himself backward, bashing Honor against the battlements. Her head hit stone, and she collapsed.

Galen reached them, but the attacker had time to draw his blade. Still dazed, Galen couldn't see the man's face clearly. His held his sword before him, but the attacker's weapon slipped under his guard. Galen felt the blade slide along his, and knew he'd misjudged fatally.

At the last moment, Honor threw herself forward, grabbed the attacker's ankle, and pulled with all her strength. The man lost his balance, lunged downward, and Galen lifted his sword. The tip pierced cloth and flesh, and the attacker impaled himself. Galen felt the weight of the body, and with instincts honed on too many battlefields, he stepped back and pulled his blade free, then pointed it at the wounded man.

His adversary dropped his weapon and clutched his belly. He stared at Galen with a surprised look, dropped to his knees, and fell facedown. Blinking to clear his vision, Galen didn't spare the dead man much of a look before whipping around to make certain there were no more opponents on the roof.

Finally his gaze found Honor, who had clawed her way to her feet and was standing there gasping and sobbing. They stared at each other in astonishment for a few moments, then Honor cried out and rushed into his arms. Galen dropped his sword and caught her, dragging her against him and pressing her head to his shoulder while she shivered and sobbed. He buried his face in her hair.

"It's over, my love. You're safe. He's dead. I won't let anything happen to you, I swear it."

Thoughts flitted through his head. This time he hadn't been too late. This time he'd saved what was most precious to him. Relief flooded through him, making his legs unsteady and his head dizzy. He held Honor even tighter and whispered a prayer of thanks.

After a while Honor stopped crying. She straightened and looked over his shoulder. He turned with her and got his first clear glimpse of the attacker's face. He looked at Honor.

"Master Baldwin? But . . ."

"H-he hated Aymer for seducing his daughter and not caring for her after she became with child." Honor drew in a long breath. "After you left I was thinking about the accounts and what you'd said about your vision, about seeing spices and bricks and hoes and such, and it came to me. Who deals with all of those things? The person who pays for them—the steward."

"Dear God, Honor."

"Baldwin kept saying how sorry he was that he had to kill me." Honor's lips trembled, but she continued. "He blamed Aymer for her death. He said if Aymer had provided for her she wouldn't have had to be a servant, and she wouldn't have fallen into that vat and been scalded to death. And, of course, he hated it that Aymer never admitted that Dagobert was his. He s-said that he didn't want to kill me, but he couldn't risk being caught."

Leaning against Galen wearily, she said, "The poor man grew demented thinking about the horror of his daughter's death and how unfair Aymer had been to Dagobert. He kept saying Dagobert could have been a nobleman."

"You're right," Galen said. "He must have been a little mad. God's mercy, Honor, I told you not to make inquiries without me. If I hadn't decided to come back here, he would have killed you. Never do something like that again." He went silent when Honor stiffened. He could see her face grow rigid and chilly.

She separated herself from him and drew an unsteady breath. "You no longer have the right to give me orders or to scold, my lord. I'm grateful to you for saving my life, but nothing else has changed between us."

"Damnation, Honor."

She regarded him with a distant gaze she wouldn't have been able to summon only a few moments ago. "I know why we never found Aymer's body."

"What?"

Honor wiped perspiration from her forehead with the sleeve of her gown. "I remembered you mentioned bricks were a part of your vision, but only after I looked again at this list." With unsteady hands she drew the scrap of parchment from her sleeve.

"You're not making sense, my love."

"Don't call me that." Honor walked toward the ladder. "I'm too weary to talk now. Baldwin followed me here and lay in wait until he saw me wander far away from you and your brothers. Then he pounced on me. He hid until your brothers went away, and then brought me here to kill me. I'm going home. We can speak more of this tomorrow."

"But tomorrow is—"

"A day like any other, thanks to you. Except that I'll have to tell Dagobert that his grandfather is dead. I'll send someone to retrieve the body in the morning."

Galen tried without success to talk to Honor several times while they retrieved the horses from Baldwin's hiding place and headed back to the castle. Sore in body, dispirited and fearful, Galen watched Honor's set features. He knew her well enough to recognize what an effort it was for her to remain calm and removed, but she did it. They reached Castle Stafford to face the curiosity of his family and Sir Walter. Honor only stayed long enough to tell them of Baldwin's death, if not the details. Then she left Galen to explain the circumstances of her long absence and ascended the stairs to her room.

It took him almost an hour to tell the story, and still there were gaps only Honor could fill. At last he was able to go up to her chamber, but to his anguish, Jacoba was standing guard outside, her chunky arms folded, a long, thick wooden spoon clutched in her hand for a weapon.

He faced the woman with a scowl that would have alarmed the most battle-hardened knight. "Out of my way."

"No use, me lord."

"Jacoba, I'm in no mood to put up with your insolence."

"I can see that," the waiting woman said, relaxing her stance. She lowered her voice. "I give her a potion to put her to sleep. She was crying and couldn't stop. Now, you just save your apologies and your begging for a while."

"She's not hurt?"

NINETEEN

Honor groaned and opened one eye. Through the bed curtains she could see bright light. It was well past prime, sunrise, and Jacoba's potion had made her sleep late. What had awakened her from that dreamless, heavy sleep? Ah, she heard it again. That great bawling laugh.

"Oh, no. Uncle Edwin."

The betrothal guests were arriving. She listened carefully and heard footsteps and the high-pitched voice of Edwin's wife, Maud. Maud had a plain name, but she had been and still was a pretty woman with a tendency to chatter.

Honor slumped under the covers with an unsteady sigh. For a brief moment she'd forgotten that her relatives would be arriving today to witness the betrothal. Hiding under the covers, Honor twitched the bed curtains aside to judge the light.

Yes, it was well past prime. Father had invited almost a dozen relatives and friends, and they'd be arriving all morning. The betrothal would take place around nones, the hour halfway between noontide and vespers.

She would have to speak to Father before then. She should get up and do it now, but she didn't want to move. It wasn't that she was sore from being attacked, bound and gagged by Master Baldwin in the forest of Durance Guarde. It wasn't the nightmare of being stuffed into an old cistern while he made an appearance at the castle. It wasn't even the ordeal of being dragged up Berengar's Tower and almost knocked on the head and thrown to her death. No, she didn't want to move because her spirit was dead.

She didn't want to face Father, her relatives, and friends, and most of all she didn't want to face Galen de Marlowe. Her heart seemed to have frozen, then cracked and splintered. Even her near escape from death hadn't encouraged it to reassemble itself.

She should be grateful to be alive. She should be in church on her knees thanking God. Mayhap she would be able to do that in a few days. Right now all she could think of was how Galen had appeared at the moment she thought was her last. How her heart had soared higher than the highest tower at Durance Guarde at the sight of him.

And then when Baldwin had tried to kill him, she'd become a monster of fury. She'd tried to kill Baldwin with her bare hands and teeth. But once Baldwin was dead, she'd come to her senses.

Galen had rescued her because any good and chivalrous knight would have done the same. She was the woman he wanted to bed, but not to wed. The woman to whom he'd been forced to make an offer by an unfortunate chance. Honor sniffed and wiped away her tears with the edge of a sheet. Today was going to be a nightmare.

A voice on the other side of the bed curtains startled her. "You got to come out of there sometime, me lady."

"Go away, Jacoba."

"Your father is asking for you. He wants to know why you began to suspect Master Baldwin after all these years. He asked Lord de Marlowe, but all he got was a funny look. So now Sir Walter wants to see you."

She had forgotten that last night she'd promised her father more details after she'd rested. They had announced to the household that Baldwin Trune's death had been an accident so as not to disgrace his innocent family. Last night she hadn't felt strong enough to do more than that, but Father wanted to understand it all. What tale was she going to tell him that wouldn't expose Galen's secret? Galen.

"False-hearted wretch," she sniffed. Groaning again, she threw back the covers and shoved the bed curtains aside.

She washed and put on her shift, then stared at the gown Jacoba held out to her. "Not that one."

"It's the one you ordered special. It came yesterday from London. The seamstress barely finished it in time."

"I don't care."

Jacoba just stood there. "I got no other ready."

"There's the yellow one."

"You burned the bodice."

"The crimson silk."

"Stepped on the hem and tore the waist."

"The emerald green damask."

"You trod in muck and I ain't been able to get the stain out yet."

"Then I'll wear one of my black ones," Honor said with her hands on her hips.

Jacoba shook her head. "I just saw the washer woman stirring them in the laundry vat.

Honor studied the waiting woman with suspicion, but Jacoba returned her stare undismayed.

"Oh, very well."

The gown was indigo, the color of her eyes, and embroidered with silver thread. It had a deep V neckline that revealed an undergown of lighter blue and silver. Honor had refused to order a hennin to match, and had planned to wear the sapphire pendant in her loose hair. Instead, she gathered her hair in a silver net at the back of her neck and ignored Jacoba's objections.

"By me faith, lady, you're the most unfashionable girl I ever did see."

"Good," Honor snapped. "Then it won't surprise you when I return to my widow's barb."

Oblivious to Jacoba's laments, Honor hiked up her skirts and stalked downstairs. It was a strain to greet Uncle Edwin, her three cousins, her father's old friend the Earl of Surrey and all the others. She avoided Galen's brothers.

Luckily her uncle Edwin and aunt Maud had appointed themselves surrogate hosts and were offering wine and wafers to all newcomers. Honor made her way over to Sir Walter, who was talking to his aged great-uncle, a blue-veined, white-haired old man sitting in her father's favorite chair, trying to stay awake.

"Ah, my dear, you're here at last. I would speak with you at once. Come with me. Excuse us for a while, Uncle. Last minute details to arrange, as you know well."

"What?" the old man asked. "Oh, go on and leave me alone, Walter."

"Galen," Sir Walter said, "come with us."

Honor whirled around to find him standing but a few paces from her. Her heart pounded, and her hands were suddenly clammy. Vertigo nearly made her stumble, but she took a deep breath and nodded to him coldly, trying not to notice his great, dark eyes, which seemed to draw her to him in spite of the fact that she knew her heart was shattered ice. Before more disturbing feelings could stir in less frozen parts of her body, Honor turned on her heel and followed her father. They met in the anteroom that adjoined Sir Walter's chamber.

"Now, daughter, you must explain to me what caused you to suspect that your husband was murdered after all these years. I accept that it must be so, or Baldwin wouldn't have tried to kill you."

"And he confessed even as he tried," she replied. "He said he didn't want to do it, but that he knew I suspected what he'd done when I questioned him in the treasury yesterday. I think guilt and God's anger had driven him a little mad."

Sir Walter shook his head. "But what brought about your suspicions?"

She glanced at Galen, who had gone to a window and was looking outside. His body was rigid, and he had dark shadows under his eyes. He turned his head and looked into her eyes. Honor was startled to find in his gaze not uneasiness, but trust. Still staring into those onyx and gold eyes, she thought quickly.

"Um, yesterday morning I overheard him in the chapel praying for forgiveness for causing Aymer's death."

Galen didn't appear surprised at her words and spoke for the first time. "Lady Honor told me he also confessed to her what he'd done with the body."

"Aye," she said, dragging her eyes from his. She turned to her father. "You see, he knew if Aymer was found, people would notice the wound on his head, so Baldwin had to hide his body. If you remember, Father, that was the year after we built the new kitchen out of stone, and Master Baldwin got the idea of adding on to it. I think we should go to the brewery at once."

The three of them left the hall, made a stop at a storeroom for a pick, and entered the brewery. Sir Walter dismissed the servants inside, and the vats of ale and beer were abandoned.

Honor walked along the wall that separated the kitchen and brewery. The vast fireplaces of each building had been placed back-to-back on either side of a thick wall.

"I recall Baldwin stopping the work on the wall early that day," Sir Walter said.

"Yes," Honor said. "But I remember it was more than half finished at the time." She faced the fireplace and pointed to the wall to the right. "See how this side has an additional thickness?"

The two men joined her in studying the difference in thickness.

While Sir Walter walked along the wall Honor moved nearer to Galen and whispered so that her father couldn't hear. "Remember the bricks you talked about?"

Galen nodded, then spoke quietly, "There's just enough space."

"About here, I think." Honor pointed to a spot in the wall.

Galen swung the pick. He hacked at the mortar and brick until he'd made a hole large enough for a child to fit through. Sir Walter pulled a loose brick out of the wall, took a candle, and held it up to the hole.

"God deliver us!" He backed away, crossing himself.

Galen took the candle from Sir Walter and looked inside a gap between the kitchen and brewery walls, then he held the light while Honor stepped forward. Steeling herself, she looked over the bricks and down at the floor where Galen pointed. She drew back at once, gasping and trying to catch her breath.

The brewery floor seemed to waver. Then she was swept up in Galen's arms. Her father's voice sounded in her ears, then the world steadied itself. Sir Walter was standing over her holding the candle while Galen held her.

"Aymer's clothes. Those were what he was wearing. There's nothing left of him but—"

"Don't say it." Galen squeezed her gently. "Remember, ashes to ashes. Dust to dust. It was over long ago."

Honor bit her lip and nodded. Swallowing hard, she struggled out of Galen's arms.

He set her on her feet, and Sir Walter put his arm around her. "By my faith, I don't know what to do."

"I must get out of this place," Honor said.

Sir Walter began to guide her away from Aymer's makeshift tomb. "Of course, my dear. You need fresh air. Let me think. God's mercy, we've all our guests to think of, and the betrothal."

"I advise you to keep silent," Galen said. "Otherwise you'll have a feud with Isidore Jennings, and he'll want blood."

"But I didn't kill Aymer," Sir Walter protested.

Galen stopped at the brewery door and regarded them with a severe expression. "It won't matter. He'll use it as a pretext to disgrace you and confiscate your lands."

They walked into the sunny warmth of the day, and Honor took deep breaths while holding on to her father's arm.

"You're right, de Marlowe. We'd best seal that hole again and wait until after the betrothal to inter poor Aymer."

Sir Walter and Galen went back into the brewery. Honor heard them stacking bricks while she waited.

The men were soon back. Sir Walter brushed mortar from his robe and Galen dusted his hands. Honor avoided looking at him even though his gaze sought hers. It was painful to be near him even when they said nothing to each other. In his presence she felt as if she would explode out of her skin.

"The hole is blocked," Sir Walter said. "Well enough for now. Sir Renard will seal it himself during the betrothal feast. I can trust him. Once the guests are gone we can make proper arrangements."

He scratched his chin. "But I must bury him. He must have the offices of the church that were denied him."

Galen walked over to Sir Walter. "Please allow me to speak to the king first."

Sir Walter bowed. "That's kind of you, de Marlowe. If you could go to London tomorrow?"

"Father," Honor said.

Galen inclined his head. "I shall do so with all speed."

Honor edged over to Sir Walter. "*Father.*"

"Your aid will save me from great peril, my son."

"Father!"

Sir Walter jumped and turned to her. "God save us, child. What ails you?"

"I must speak privily to you before we do anything, Father."

"Honor, don't," Galen said.

"Galen," Sir Walter said, pointing to Aunt Maud, who had come out of the hall and was waving. "I believe my sister wants to speak with you."

"Of course, but—"

"Best do her bidding," Sir Walter said. "She wants to quiz you about your family and property, and she won't go away until she's satisfied."

"You might as well leave," Honor said without looking at him. "I will do this should the king himself try to prevent me."

Sir Walter looked at her with startled curiosity, but Galen didn't move.

"No matter what you tell him, it's not finished," he said.

"You're wrong." Honor turned to Sir Walter. "Father, I need air after seeing Aymer's—after seeing Aymer. Would you take me up to the wall walk?"

"Certainly, my dear."

Without looking back, she entered the nearest tower and began the climb to the wall walk. Once outside again, she deliberately stepped to the battlements and gazed out over the countryside, even though she didn't see the fields of ripening wheat and barley.

Her father was slower, but he was at her side before she was ready to speak. She watched a shepherd and his dog driving a flock to a distant meadow. Finally she faced Sir Walter.

"Father, I do not wish to marry Galen de Marlowe."

"Not wish—what's this?" Sir Walter was already turning red. "Why, yesterday you were dancing about the place like a virgin on May Day."

"I don't wish to speak of my reasons. I will only say that Lord de Marlowe has most grievously offended me, and I can't marry him."

Her father was gawking at her, openmouthed. "It suffices not, this grievous offense, whatever it is. First you say you're a vowess and will not marry. Then you say you will have Galen de Marlowe, one of the most influential men in the kingdom.

And now you say you won't have him at all. Yes, no, yes, no. Bah!"

"Now, Father."

"No, by my faith. All lovers quarrel. Husbands and wives disagree. Arguments are soon mended when ill-humors fade."

"It's not a lovers' quarrel."

Sir Walter shook his head. He began to pace and mutter.

"After all this trouble, after the king himself has taken notice and given his consent. No, my dear, no. It won't do. Mortally offend Galen de Marlowe? It's not to be considered."

Honor grabbed her father's sleeve, tears making her vision blurry.

"Father, I can't marry him."

Sir Walter's voice grew louder. "And why not? Because he has annoyed you? Madness. I've had enough of your changeable ways, daughter. You're in love with that man, and you're going to marry him."

"But he doesn't love me," Honor whispered, her tears falling at last. Her throat hurt from trying to keep them back. She covered her face with her hands. "He doesn't love me."

Sir Walter put his arm around her shoulders. "Now, child, don't cry. Whatever the matter may be, I'm sure it can be settled if you talk to him."

"No!" Honor sprang away from him. "I don't want to talk to him."

"God give me patience," Sir Walter said. "Very

well, don't talk to him. But you're still going to take your part in the betrothal ceremony."

Honor wiped her eyes and shook her head.

"I know that look," Sir Walter said. "You're planning some mischief, but I won't have it."

Her father looked over her shoulder and signaled to a guard at the next tower. The man came running.

"Alfred, escort Lady Honor to her chamber and make sure she stays there until I send for her."

"Aye, Sir Walter."

"I'll send George and Nigel to stand guard with you as well."

Honor was staring at her father in horror. "You're not going to do this."

"You'll recover your senses once the betrothal ceremony is over," Sir Walter said. "Go, Alfred, and if she escapes you, I'll hang you by your heels from the kitchen steeple."

Honor opened her mouth to protest, but Sir Walter glared at Alfred, who took her arm and guided her away with a grip so firm that Honor had no choice but to leave. A few minutes later she watched her chamber door shut and heard Alfred place a bar across it.

Honor sat on a chest at the foot of the bed and stared at the panel, stunned. Why didn't her father understand? Why was he being so obstinate? Couldn't he see how greatly she objected to Galen de Marlowe?

Mayhap he couldn't understand. Men looked at

the world differently than women, and Father had been so happy with Mother. No doubt he imagined her being as contented with Galen.

Honor flushed with humiliation at the contrast between her parents' marriage and what she would endure. Well, she wouldn't endure it—a marriage in which Galen would pity her for loving him when he did not love her. She grew ill thinking of it.

Honor rose and paced the floor. Father was going to see to it that she went to the betrothal ceremony. What he couldn't do was make her say the vows. When the time came, she would simply refuse. It would be ungracious and create ill feeling and evil report, but she had no other choice. The alternative was to betroth herself to Galen, to promise before God that she would marry him.

That was the nature of the betrothal, to signify before the Lord one's future intention to marry. In fact, there was little difference in the wording between the two ceremonies. In a betrothal the priest used what the church called words of the future. He asked, "Do you promise that you will take this man to husband if the Holy Church consents?" In marriage, the priest asked, "Do you take this man to husband?"

Honor clenched her fists as she considered what she was about to do. She would humiliate Galen before many witnesses. He had hurt her, but she found that she no longer wished to hurt him in return. The terrible events of last night had burned away her lust for revenge. But she'd be damned before she'd take a man who'd been forced to marry her.

Honor sat down on the chest again and sighed. She was exhausted and suffering a pain she feared would never leave her. All she wanted was to be left alone.

So, in a few hours, when the priest asked, she would simply reply, "I will not."

TWENTY

As the hour of nones approached, Honor sat on her bed and pretended to read one of her new books, a translation of Virgil. Jacoba bustled about unpacking and setting new volumes on a special shelf. Honor read the same sentence for the fifth time, closed the book and set it aside. She pulled her knees to her chest and rested her chin on them.

"Me lady, please. You're going to ruin that beautiful gown. Look, it's all covered with dust. I declare before God I don't know how you can get so dirty in so short a time."

"Never mind that," Honor said. "You're certain Dagobert isn't too upset about his grandfather?"

"He hardly ever saw Master Baldwin, me lady, what with him being in service to you so far away from here. He's in good spirits today because he's proud to be a part of the ceremony. Later, when we have the funeral, he'll begin to understand and grow sad."

Honor thought for a while, then said, "We might be able to bribe Alfred and the others to let us escape."

Jacoba set her fists on her hips and shook her head.

"Sir Walter's threatened them right furious. Says if they let you out, he'll throw them all in the dungeon."

"Father hasn't used the dungeon in years. He just locks thieves and criminals in the shed next to the piggery."

Jacoba wiped dust off a packing crate with a rag. "Sir Walter says he's found the key to the dungeon. Showed it to Alfred special."

"Humph. It won't do him any good. I may have to go to the ceremony, but I don't have to consent. So it's no use."

"Faith, but you're a stubborn girl. Always were. I remember what a time your mother used to have."

"Oh, not now, Jacoba."

Someone rapped on the door.

"It must be time," Honor said as she got off the bed.

Jacoba rushed over to her and began brushing Honor's gown, sending clouds of mortar dust into the air. Honor coughed and waved her hands.

"That's enough, Jacoba."

Sir Walter's firm voice came through the door. "Daughter?"

"What," Honor said, nearly growling.

"Are you ready?"

"No."

"That's nice." The door opened, and Sir Walter stood there smiling fixedly, dressed in red and black velvet. Behind him stood Uncle Edwin and Aunt Maud, both with the same kind of smile, as if they'd been printed on their faces with a press.

"Come, daughter. It's past time. Everyone is waiting."

"Let them wait," Honor said with a chilly smile of her own. "I won't be forced to take a man I don't want."

Sir Walter beamed at her. "God save us, my dear, but you're all a-jitter. I told Edwin and Maud you'd taken fright as if this were your first marriage. They understand."

"I'm not frightened," Honor ground out between her teeth.

She glared at her father, but he kept beaming at her. He took hold of her arm and marched her out of the room. Everyone followed, including Alfred, Nigel, and George. Dagobert waited at the top of the chapel steps smiling with pride at his role in the ceremony. He puffed out his thin chest, opened the doors and marched inside.

Sir Walter followed the page, and didn't release

Honor until he'd guided her down the aisle between the seated guests to stand before the chaplain and Theodoric. When she reached the altar Honor scowled at the de Marlowe brothers sitting in the first row, then looked around the chapel for the first time. She turned to her father.

"Where is Lord de Marlowe?"

Sir Walter's determined smile faltered. His questioning gaze darted to Simon de Marlowe, who made a helpless gesture.

"My dear," Sir Walter said.

She turned to look at the de Marlowes, but they stared at the altar, at the stained-glass windows, everywhere but at her. Her gaze focused on the quiet one.

"You," she said, her voice echoing off the fan-vaulted roof. "Fulk, where is Lord de Marlowe?" Whispers started in the rows on either side of the aisle.

Fulk glanced at his brothers, hesitated, then rose and approached her as he would an angry lioness. His steps were slow, and his bow long, but at last he faced her and spoke so softly she couldn't hear him.

"Speak up, Fulk."

Instead, he drew nearer. His fingers twisted in his gilded belt; he toyed with the braid on his doublet.

"I'm waiting," Honor snapped.

"He said he'd be back."

"He left," she said faintly. The chapel receded, and when it returned she found that she was holding on to Fulk's arm for support.

Their gazes locked, and she watched his grow shadowy. Then he winced as if in pain, and a shuttered look came over him. Honor gave his reaction little more than a passing thought, for her own pain consumed her. She was the one who was supposed to do the refusing. Instead, her private humiliation had been dragged into the light and displayed before her closest companions, and others who would spread the tale throughout the kingdom. Everyone would know that the great Galen de Marlowe had run away rather than marry her.

Fulk was holding her wrist now and speaking in a low, urgent tone. "I know my brother. He wouldn't leave if it weren't a matter of utmost gravity."

"I'm certain," Honor said, disengaging her wrist and stepping back from him. "The matter of utmost gravity is escaping the horror of having to marry me."

"No, you don't understand."

Honor held up her hand. "I fear I do. He knew I was going to refuse him during the ceremony, so he chose to reject me first. Your brother is a coward, my lord."

Fulk tried to speak, but she turned her back on him and confronted her father.

"Lord de Marlowe isn't here, and you let me walk into this chapel anyway, Father. How could you do that?"

Sir Walter waved his hands. "What could I do? Everyone was waiting in here. He rode off saying he'd return, that we should wait for him. He'll be here any moment."

"I do not purpose to stand here waiting like some beggar seeking sanctuary." Honor lifted her chin and raised her voice so that everyone in the chapel could hear her.

"It seems Lord de Marlowe has saved me the unpleasant task of refusing to betroth myself to him. I am pleased, but I regret that you good gentles have been put to trouble for nothing. For this I beg your pardons most heartily."

Honor sank into a deep curtsey and sailed out of the chapel. She was halfway to the hall when Jacoba caught up with her. Dagobert appeared in Jacoba's wake.

"Me lady, what are you doing?" the waiting woman asked.

"We're leaving, Jacoba. At once." She ran up the steps and into the great hall, where the servants were in the midst of preparations for the betrothal feast.

Jacoba hurried after Honor up the stairs, with Dagobert close behind.

The page was excited. "Where are we going, me lady?"

"To Florence."

"Florence!" Dagobert clapped his hands and laughed while Jacoba muttered and shook her head.

"But first we'll go to Mainz, in Germany, to buy another printer's press." Honor yanked open the door to her chamber and clapped her hands. Two serving maids answered her summons. "Everyone pack at once. We're leaving upon the morrow, at sunrise. Don't gawk at me. Make haste."

"Oh, me lady, your father won't approve," Jacoba said.

"No doubt my father will still be in the chapel waiting for Lord de Marlowe as I ride over the drawbridge. It doesn't signify." Honor turned on the waiting woman and pointed at her. "Mark my words, Jacoba. Upon the morrow we begin the journey to the Continent, and God help the soul who tries to stop me."

THE NEXT MORNING Honor was in the outer ward checking her mare's saddle girth. Sir Walter stood by, surveying the coach and wagons strung out behind the mare. His impassive expression broke into a resentful one each time he glanced at the de Marlowes, who had decided to escort Honor as far as the cutoff that led to Argent. Honor knew hard words had passed between him and Simon de Marlowe, but her father wouldn't speak of it.

"You should ride in the coach, my dear. Ladies ride in coaches."

Honor tugged on a stirrup and said, "Ladies who

ride in coaches get bounced about like dried peas in a shaken bottle."

She turned to her father and saw his grief-stricken expression. She managed a smile and blinked back tears. Last night had been filled with bad dreams, and this leave-taking had been in one of them. She kissed his cheek and whispered to him, "I'll be well, Father. I promise. I've got Sir Renard and his men to protect me, and once I'm in France Lorenzo de Medici will send an escort. I've already sent ahead with a message."

"I know, my dear, but I did so wish to see you happy. I was certain that de Marlowe loved—Well." He sighed. "It's God's will, I'm sure."

Honor looked away. "Yes. Although it's obviously Galen's will as well."

"He's a fool," Sir Walter said with a doting look. "You're the finest, prettiest woman a man could pray for."

Honor bit her lip and forced back more tears. "Dear Father, I shall miss you so."

Sir Walter threw his arms around her and squeezed so hard she gasped. Then he kissed her forehead. Somehow that kiss made Honor's world a tiny bit brighter.

She gave him a faint smile, and he helped her mount. Sir Renard gave the signal, and the outriders rode under the portcullis. The little caravan began to move. Sir Walter walked with her to the drawbridge, kissed her hand and let it go.

"I'll bring back pomegranate trees for Perkin to plant," she called as she rode into the shadow of the bridge.

"And olive trees too!" Sir Walter said. "I shall enjoy watching him try to keep them alive in winter."

As she rode out of the castle, Simon de Marlowe and his brothers caught up with her, and Honor found herself surrounded. She needn't have worried. None of them spoke to her. They seemed as mystified as everyone else at Galen's disappearance.

"You needn't feel obliged to accompany me the whole way," she said after about an hour. She pointed to the looming forest they were about to enter. "We'll part on the other side of the forest, in any case. Please feel free to ride on now."

Simon shook his head. "We can't leave you in the forest, my lady."

"Although," Macaire said with a wry look, "you seem to know it better than we do."

"Indeed," Honor said with a distant tone. She wanted to be rid of these men. She was sick of the whole de Marlowe family.

They rode into the forest without further exchanges, and soon they were deep in the midst of old gnarled trees whose canopy dimmed the sunlight. Tiny beams of light pierced the gloom, and as noontide approached, Sir Renard sent more men riding out at the flanks of their party as a precaution. Honor didn't interfere, although she doubted there was much to fear from bandits or noblemen of evil repute. The forest still kept its perilous reputation, and they were too near Durance Guarde, where few outlaws wished to lurk.

They crossed a fast-running stream, and Honor caught a glimpse of an ivy-shrouded, crumbling tower. She returned her gaze to the path and kept it there. She prevented herself from thinking miserable thoughts by planning the stops on her journey to Mainz. Then, abruptly, Fabron pulled his horse out of line and kicked it into a gallop, disappearing down the path.

Simon hauled on his reins. "I knew it." He rode after his brother. As he vanished into the trees, his brothers also pulled out of line and rode off.

Sir Renard turned his horse around and rode back to Honor. "Is anything wrong, my lady?"

"Fabron suddenly bolted, and the rest chased after him. I suspect they couldn't endure the embarrassment any longer. After all, their honor has been touched by their brother's disgrace."

"I'm sorry, my lady."

Pain jabbed at her chest, and she said hastily, "Please. Don't speak of it."

"Aye, my lady."

Sir Renard rode back to the head of the caravan, and Honor was left to herself. She was fighting against a wall of anguish that threatened to collapse upon her. She couldn't let it bury her.

Without warning the memory of Galen's gentle, dark eyes came to her. She felt his touch on her skin. She bathed in the heat of his body, felt the titillation his wicked smile evoked.

"Oh, no," she said to herself. "You're not going to pine, Honor Jennings. I forbid you to pine after a dishonorable wretch." She sped up, passing Sir Renard at a trot. "I'll ride ahead a little and come back directly."

"Not too far, my lady."

She waved, and cantered past the outriders. The faster she rode the faster she wanted to go, and soon she was galloping recklessly down the winding path. It seemed that if she could go fast enough, she could outrun her unhappiness. Her lungs worked harder and harder, and her mare began to foam at the mouth from exertion. Finally she reached the edge of the forest, glimpsed an expanse of light, and burst out of the shadows.

The first thing she saw was a line of men ranged across the road in front of her. She pulled hard on the reins. The mare slowed sharply, then rose on her hind legs and pawed the air.

Honor brought her under control, pulling firmly on the reins and speaking softly. The animal danced back and forth, then settled. Honor kept her eyes on the men, squinting against the harsh sunlight. One of them separated himself from the rest and rode toward her. Honor shaded her eyes, looked harder.

"By the Trinity. Galen." She hauled on the reins again, spinning her horse around, and plunged back toward the forest.

"Honor, stop!"

She slapped the mare with the reins and the animal surged forward. Only a few yards to go, and she could lose herself in the forest. Dirt sprayed in her face as the mare's hooves dug into the soil. She could see the shadows clearly now. Almost there.

She was so fixed on gaining the shelter of the trees that she didn't see Galen's nearness until he was beside her. His giant stallion loomed over her mare. Galen leaned sideways, trying to grasp the smaller horse's bridle. He missed, swore and grabbed Honor around the waist instead.

Honor felt herself plucked from the saddle and deposited in Galen's lap. She slipped, cried out and threw her arms around his neck. Out of breath, she couldn't even protest until Galen had slowed his horse and walked him into the shadows at the edge of the forest.

Once the stallion stopped, Honor writhed in Galen's grasp and slid to the ground. She landed in a heap, with her skirt over her head. She heard him chuckle as she fought her way out of the tangle and rounded on him. Red-faced and speechless with wrath, she ran at him and punched him in the stomach.

"Ugh."

Honor ignored him while he bent over and

clutched his stomach. Her fury was so great she feared she would expire from it. She walked swiftly around in circles, muttering curses and kicking dead branches and stones. She ended up back in front of Galen, still breathless.

"I swear you're the most God-cursed foul-hearted spawn of the devil ever born to woman. You're more callous and cruel than Aymer ever was."

"Honor, listen, I didn't mean to—"

"Shut your mouth," Honor said. She wiped her brow with the sleeve of her gown. Her chest heaving, she glanced over her shoulder to see that Galen's brothers were still waiting where she'd first seen them. "The king will hear of your evil deeds, my lord. I care not that he calls you friend. Mayhap after this, he will not."

She would have gone on, but Galen lunged at her and clamped his hand over her mouth. Honor bit it. He yelped and withdrew his hand, shaking it.

"Damn it, you little wretch. That hurt."

"Good. I hope I broke the skin. I hope the wound festers and rots and makes your hand fall off. If I'm favored by fortune, the rot will spread up your arm and to your head. Not that you aren't rotten already. May all the devils in hell draw your soul to Satan."

She stopped when Galen suddenly turned his back and walked to his horse. Was he going to leave her here?

"Stop this moment, you pestilence of a man."

Galen ignored her. He reached his horse, and Honor charged after him. When she reached him he was untying a bag attached to his saddle.

"You left me to face everyone at the chapel, you black-hearted knave!"

Turning around, Galen thrust the bag at Honor so that she was forced to grasp it. She stumbled backward, then looked down at the leather satchel, scowling.

"Open it."

She held it out to him. "I want nothing of yours."

"It's not mine. It's yours."

The bag was growing heavy so she dropped it, and regarded him with contempt. "Aymer used to give me gifts after he'd done something mean. It always meant he wanted me to do something, like play hostess to some king's man whose favor he was courting." She walked around Galen, studying him as if he were an ill-favored stallion for sale. "What do you want this time, my lord?"

"Honor, I beg you to listen."

"You didn't answer me." She stopped in front of him and gave him a cool stare. "What is it you want this time?"

"If you would but listen a moment, my love."

"Don't call me your love. I was never your love, and I'm through listening to you."

She turned her back on him and walked three steps before he caught her hand. She yanked it free and rounded on him.

"By God's mercy, if you touch me again I shall scratch your eyes out."

Galen backed up, opening his arms and shaking his head. "I yield. I yield, but in return you must promise to hear what I have to say."

"Be quick. I'm weary of your presence, my lord."

"Do you know why I was at Durance Guarde?"

Honor frowned. "I care not."

"I was hiding, and enduring a most malevolent vision. One that involves the royal family. There, now you can destroy me with few words."

Honor could think of nothing to say. Galen took a cautious step toward her and continued.

"I felt drawn to Durance Guarde, and I was sure it was because I needed solitude in which to make sense of the vision."

Quietly he described the vision, and when he finished she still had no words for him. He had trusted her with this dangerous confidence, but she'd been hurt too badly to return his trust.

"Good. At least you haven't run away yet," he said. "Because I was wrong about why I was drawn to Durance Guarde."

"Indeed," she said, grateful that her voice was steady and cool.

"It had nothing to do with the Tower vision." He took another step toward her and said, "I was confusing two visions, Honor. One of evil, and one of good—most marvelous, wondrous good. Don't you see? I was drawn to Durance Guarde because of you."

"What?" She regarded him with bewilderment.

"I could have taken refuge at Argent, but I was drawn to that overgrown ruin of a place. And always when I thought of it I experienced this pleasurable excitement and anticipation. I thought I was seeking refuge, my love, when all the time, I was seeking you. I thank God I listened to that particular vision without realizing what I was doing." He reached her at last and knelt, holding her eyes with his. "I thank God for it."

Honor stared at him, then she absently shoved a wisp of hair out of her eyes. "Lovely words, my lord, but you have a gift for fine words."

"Then judge me by my actions." He nodded at the discarded leather satchel.

Honor hesitated, then went to it, knelt and unlaced the ties that held it shut. Inside was a parcel wrapped in thick cloth and twine. She unwrapped it to find a box made of mahogany with gilded fittings and a lock. Galen came over to kneel beside her. She eyed him warily, but he was only holding out a key.

"This isn't mine," she said. "You've made a mistake." Her eyes narrowed. "No doubt you've confused me with one of your other ladyloves."

Galen shook his head and smiled. "I told you, I'm not confused any longer, my little sunset. Open it."

"You're not going away until I do, are you?"

"No."

Honor snatched the key. Giving him another

mistrustful look, she inserted it in the lock and opened the box. The lid swung back to reveal dozens of compartments of varying sizes. In each compartment lay piles of small, narrow metal bars. Honor's breath caught. She picked up one of the little bars and held it between her thumb and forefinger. She breathed in uneven little gusts.

Looking up at Galen, she said, "This is a type case."

"Yes."

"Full of type. A complete set of type. For a printer's press."

"Yes."

She pulled out a lower drawer in the box to reveal a different set of type.

"That's a set called Italic," he said. "It's much easier to read than the type Master Caxton uses."

Speechless, Honor looked from the type case to Galen. He was smiling at her still, but her thoughts seemed to have vanished, and she just knelt there staring at him. When she didn't move, he reached past her and pulled another object from the bag. It looked like a giant mushroom with a handle on top.

"This is the printer's ball. I couldn't carry the rest. It's still in the wagon on its way from London."

Honor wet her lips. "What's still on its way?"

"Your printer's press, of course."

"Press," she repeated mindlessly. "My printer's press sank."

"And I got you another," he replied.

"But, but . . ." Confusion had replaced every thought in her head now.

"I had a friend in London pay a rival of Master Caxton's ten times its worth. He can buy another, if he doesn't decide to retire before he even starts printing."

Honor replaced the type and closed the box. "My press?"

"Certainly. What would I want with it?"

"You left to fetch the type case."

"Forgive me, love. I had to ride much farther than I thought to meet the wagon that's transporting the cursed thing."

"You must have sent for the press the moment you heard mine sank," Honor said, clutching the ink ball.

Galen took the ink ball and set it aside, then kissed her hand and brought it to his cheek. Honor looked at him, still stunned.

"Now that I have you speechless, you must listen to me. For so long I've been afraid that I would make another terrible mistake and cause harm to someone I love. Then I met you, and you wouldn't go away. You became a part of my soul before I knew it. I tried for so long to deny what was happening. Even when I knew I didn't want to live without you, I refused to admit it to myself. And then that vision of Aymer's death came upon me while I was with you, because of you."

Galen took both her hands in his. "I used that

cursed vision as an excuse to do what I wanted all along, to claim you."

"You did?"

He nodded urgently. "I realized it too late. I can be most grievously headstrong, you know. And because of my blindness, I hurt you. I beg you to forgive me." He leaned closer and said, "I love you, Honor Jennings. Please don't send me away."

It was as if those frozen ice shards into which her heart had shattered reassembled themselves in an instant. Her whole body warmed, and euphoria spread from her heart to her fingertips and toes. Honor shrieked and threw herself at Galen. At the impact, he fell backward and she landed on top of him. She kissed him hard, and his arms wrapped around her.

Honor submerged into an ocean of glowing happiness, only to lift her lips from Galen's and say, "I told no one about the visions. Even when I hated you. Did you really buy a whole printer's press? Where shall we put it? Oh, we must find Sir Renard and go back home."

"Saints, Brother, does she always babble like that?"

Honor looked up to find Simon de Marlowe riding up, along with Galen's other siblings.

Galen appeared undisturbed. He lifted Honor off him, stood and helped her up.

"No, Simon." Galen brushed Honor's grass-stained gown. "But she's often a mess."

Honor caught his hand. "At least I'm no Leekshanks."

Galen grinned at her even though his brothers began to snigger at him. Honor glanced down at the type case, then up at Galen.

"What would you have done if your gift hadn't softened my heart?"

He pulled her close and whispered in her ear, "I would have spirited you away to Durance Guarde. Then I would have waited for you to trip over a tree root and rescued you. You know what happens when you trip. We end up on the ground—"

"I forgive you! Just don't go on." Honor blushed at the curious looks from Galen's brothers.

Galen bowed. "As my lady wishes. Shall we go?" He lifted her hand to his lips. "I'm grievously late, my love, but will you come to the betrothal ceremony with me?"

"I will, my lord," Honor said softly. "With all my heart, I will."

EPILOGUE

⎯⎯◇ London, Christmas, 1476

IN THE PALACE of Westminster Honor sat on a bench beside the fireplace in the room assigned to her by the king. Although Jacoba had put fresh logs on the fire, a draft whisked under the door and up her skirt, so Honor curled sideways on the bench and lifted her feet off the floor. She stared into the flames while resting her chin on her knees. She was waiting for Galen.

She had finally persuaded him to warn the king about the danger his vision seemed to predict for little Edward and Richard, the royal princes, but Galen had been gone for a long time. The door swung open, and Jacoba came in with a tray, goblets, and a flagon.

"Hippocras, me lady. It will warm you. And I

brought a bit of that roast swan that was done for the feast last night."

Honor smiled, but then she shivered. "Close the door. I'm freezing."

Jacoba set the tray down and went to shut the door, but she almost rammed it into Galen as he tried to cross the threshold. "Oh, dear. Pray forgive me, me lord." Jacoba opened the door and bobbed a deep curtsey. "Are you all right, me lord?"

Galen eyed Jacoba. "No harm done."

"Are you certain, me lord? I'm so sorry, me lord."

"Jacoba, I would much prefer it if you'd return to your old way of treating me. Even if I've married your mistress, I don't think I can endure your kindness much longer."

Honor hid her smile by ducking her head. Jacoba's mouth worked, then she sighed.

"Oh, thank you, me lord. All them manners and politeness was about to kill me."

"You're most welcome," Galen said as he poured two goblets of heated wine and brought one to Honor.

Jacoba began to whistle happily and bustled out of the room.

"You've made her quite content," Honor said as she sipped her wine.

Galen sank down on the carpet beneath her, took a long drink of wine and glanced up at her. "Five months of being treated like royalty was almost unendurable."

"And what of your audience with the king?" Honor asked.

"I told him as much as I could without revealing the vision." Galen's head rested against her, and she stroked his gleaming hair. "Unfortunately, Edward is all too familiar with the danger to any claimant to the throne of England. He thanked me and said he could trust his wife's relatives to protect the boys."

"She does have five brothers, seven sisters, and two sons by her first husband. That's a lot of Woodvilles."

Galen shook his head. "You don't understand, my little sunset. Neither the Yorkists nor the Lancastrians have much use for the Woodvilles. Edward married a commoner and promoted too many of her family over the heads of the great magnates. He manages to keep a fine balance between all the factions, but someday he may stumble. By God's mercy, I wish I knew from whom to expect the threat."

"But you don't," Honor replied. "The vision didn't tell you that. It could come from either of the king's brothers. After all, the Duke of Clarence sided with Warwick when he rebelled, and the Duke of Gloucester doesn't trust the Woodvilles. He's as ruthless a man as I've ever met."

"And there's always the house of Lancaster," Galen said.

"Ah, yes, the red rose may destroy the white."

"Not while their claimant, Henry Tudor, is in

exile." Galen furrowed his brow. "No, I think the danger lies close. Here in England." He took another sip of hippocras and set his goblet aside. "I've done what I could to see that the boys are protected. I must be content with that, and vigilance. It may be that I'm powerless to prevent their fate, but I hope not. In any case, the vision of the Tower is gone."

Honor twisted around and slipped to the carpet, where she knelt to face him. "Are you certain it's gone?"

"Oh, yes. Another has taken its place."

"God's mercy," Honor whispered. She took him by the shoulders and studied his face, but Galen seemed calm. "You're smiling."

"Not all my visions consist of images of impending evil."

"Oh." Honor sighed her relief.

Galen kissed her, and she forgot about visions.

"Don't you want to know about the vision?"

"Hmm? Of course."

Taking her face in his hands, he kissed her nose, then her lips. "I saw it only for an instant. A young woman in a solar with two babes, a boy and a girl."

Honor sucked in her breath, staring into his dark, shining eyes. Then she scowled and batted him on the arm.

"Galen de Marlowe, you've spoiled everything."

"I thought you'd be pleased," he said, looking aggrieved.

She jumped up and planted her hands on her

hips. "Is this the way it will be? Can I never surprise you? *I* wanted to tell you. *I* wanted to see your face when I told you, and now I discover you even know it will be twins and that they will be a boy and a girl."

"I'm sorry. I didn't think you knew yet."

Honor threw up her hands. "I was waiting to be certain, you foolish man. It's only been a few weeks."

Galen knelt at her feet, took her hand and kissed it. Honor frowned at him, but he turned her hand over and kissed the palm. By the time he was kissing her wrist, she'd forgiven him.

"I promise not to spoil your surprises anymore," he said as he rose to kiss her neck.

"See that you don't," Honor said unsteadily. There was a knock at the door, and she freed her mouth long enough to say, "Go away, Jacoba."

"Yes, me lady."

Honor grabbed Galen's hand and pulled him toward the bed. "Come, my lord. By my troth, I'm sure I can find some way to surprise you this evening."

HISTORICAL NOTE

THE MID-FIFTEENTH-CENTURY battles between rival claimants to the English throne are known as the Wars of the Roses, after the red rose of the house of Lancaster and the white rose of the house of York. This sporadic warfare and political intrigue eventually put Edward, earl of March, on the throne as Edward IV. After a few internal struggles the last decade of Edward's reign—during which this novel is set—was relatively peaceful.

Edward died early at the age of forty on April 9, 1483. He left two sons, Edward V, who was twelve, and Richard, duke of York, who was nine. Their uncle Richard, duke of Gloucester, had good reason to fear for his life at the hands of the boys' maternal relatives, and he seized the throne soon after his brother died. He lodged the princes in the Tower of London. Soon rumors began to spread that the princes had been murdered, and Richard didn't produce the boys to disprove the tales. Today most historians believe that they were indeed murdered in August 1483.

The murders gained Richard III little, however. His enemies lent their support to the rival Lancastrian claimant to the throne, Henry Tudor. Henry defeated Richard at the Battle of Bosworth Field on August 22, 1485. The new king then married Edward IV's eldest daughter, Elizabeth, thus joining the red rose with the white, and effectively ending the Wars of the Roses.

About the Author

SUZANNE ROBINSON has a doctoral degree in anthropology, with a specialty in ancient Middle Eastern archaeology. She has now turned her attention to the creation of the fascinating fictional characters in her unforgettable historical romances.

Suzanne lives in San Antonio with her husband and her two English springer spaniels. She divides her time between writing historical romances and mysteries under her first name, Lynda.